Book Two *in the*
LAS VEGAS
SINNERS
Series

FULL STRENGTH

KATIE KENYHERCZ
author of On the Fly

Wishing you
love, hugs, and hockey!

Katie Kenyhercz

CRIMSON
ROMANCE
F+W Media, Inc.

Published by
Crimson Romance
an imprint of F+W Media, Inc.
10151 Carver Road, Suite 200
Blue Ash, OH 45242. U.S.A.
www.crimsonromance.com

ISBN 10: 1-4405-7575-4
ISBN 13: 978-1-4405-7575-4
eISBN 10: 1-4405-7574-6
eISBN 13: 978-1-4405-7574-7

This is a work of fiction. Names, characters, corporations, institutions, organizations, events, or locales in this novel are either the product of the author's imagination or, if real, used fictitiously. The resemblance of any character to actual persons (living or dead) is entirely coincidental.

Cover art ©123rf.com; ©istockphoto.com/jgareri

This one's for my mom, my very first reader,
and the most loving and selfless person I know. I love you!

Chapter One

Allie released a deep breath and straightened the framed degrees on the wall. Silence settled so thick, she could almost hear her heartbeat. It was hard to tell if it was a blessing or a curse being sequestered in the basement. On one hand, players would have one less excuse to avoid her because she was right next to the locker room. On the other hand, having no windows felt a little like being buried alive. The few landscape paintings at least gave the illusion of nature and made it more bearable.

A light knock on her office door made her tense, but she forced her shoulders down before she turned around to face her guest. Her heart beat double time, but it slowed when her boss stepped inside instead of her first patient.

Jacey Phlynn, owner of the Las Vegas Sinners, looked put together as usual in a black skirt suit and emerald silk blouse. As Jacey closed the door, Allie caught a glimpse of her red-soled pumps. Louboutin. She felt self-conscious in her JC Penney knockoffs, but three degrees didn't come cheap.

"Allie, I'm glad I caught you early. I know you're good on Reese's history, but I wanted to give you a heads-up—"

"He doesn't want to do this."

Jacey's eyes widened, her mouth fell open, and she shook her head.

Allie could see her boss scrambling for a polite denial, and she laughed. "It's okay. I would have rather peeled my skin off with a cheese grater than see my first shrink after my injury."

"That's right. I'm sorry. I'm sure you know exactly what to say. I wish I did."

"Let me guess. He paid you a visit; tried to get out of it."

Jacey sighed, pressed her lips together.

"It's all right. He needs this whether he knows it or not."

"I just—he may say things. Seem uncooperative. He hasn't been himself since it happened. He's a great goalie and a huge asset to this team, but if he can't get past this, we might have to trade him, and I don't want to do that. He's surgically attached to my husband. We're talking shared organs. If separated, one or both might not survive. But now that Carter's involved with the business side of the team, he has to see things as a GM would—even if that means trading his best friend. If there's any way to avoid that, I have to try."

Allie smiled as she remembered press pictures of Shane Reese with his best friend and ex-captain, Carter Phlynn. The two had played together their entire careers. Phlynn's had ended just last season with a concussion. Hard to believe *he* didn't need some therapy, too. "Reese's recovery will depend on him, but I'll do everything I can to get him there."

"Bless you. We are … *I* am so glad to have you here. Thank you again for starting on such short notice."

"I'm happy to be here. I'm excited to work with this team."

Jacey's barely suppressed laughter wasn't reassuring. Especially when she followed it up with, "Hold that thought."

• • •

"Hey, Reese. You ready to talk about your feelings?"

"Shut up." Shane Reese ignored Kevin Scott, his teammate and tormentor. Instead, he stared at the cement block wall while his friends dressed for practice. The twentieth practice he'd miss.

"Leave him alone, Scotty. Bad enough as it is."

"Thanks, Cole. Big help." Shane glanced at the hotshot rookie, Dylan Cole, who earned captaincy in his second NHL season and tried to rein in his anger. That's what got him into this mess in the first place. Cole gave him the innocent act and held up his hands. Nine years younger, and the kid thought he was Yoda or something.

Reese rolled his eyes and pushed off the bench. "Whatever. Guess I should get it over with."

"Hey, before you go … got you these." Scott turned from his locker and tossed him a box of tissues. Reese ground his teeth and threw the box back. Hard. It hit Scott between the shoulders but bounced off, harmless. The asshole was laughing.

"All right, that's enough," Cole broke in. "Scotty, hit the ice before Coach sees you missing. If you're the last out again, she'll give you a speech that'll make your ears bleed. And mine, so spare me. Reese, go talk to the doc. It won't be that bad."

"That's why you're captain, Cole. Your speeches are so damn inspiring." And before he could get another one, Reese stormed from the locker room. It would have been more dramatic without the limp, and that made him angrier. High ankle sprain. It was such a stupid injury. If that ass Chekov hadn't landed on him like that, he wouldn't be indefinitely benched at the start of the playoffs.

He had to consciously unclench his fists as he stopped at the dark wood door with the newly minted plaque. Dr. Alexandra Kallen, Sports Psychologist. He could just imagine what she looked like. Gray hair in a tight bun. Librarian glasses. Judging smirk and zero idea of what he was going through. He summoned some resolve and knocked.

"It's open."

The voice didn't *sound* old. He stepped inside, and could only stare. Alexandra Kallen was no librarian. A fitted, short sleeve, red blouse played off the coloring of dark brown hair that fell in straight layers a few inches past her shoulders. She looked more co-ed than doctor in her leg-hugging, dark denim pants and high heels that put her even with his chin. When he took her extended hand, her skin felt soft, but her grip firm. "You don't look old enough to be a doctor."

"Thank you, but I'm twenty-eight."

"Sure you don't mean eighteen?"

She arched a brow. "You're one to talk. You have your driver's license yet?"

"You don't sound like a doctor either."

She laughed, and when her features relaxed, she looked even younger. "Thanks, I think. You're Shane Reese? It's nice to meet you."

"I, uh, you too. Um, what should I call you? Dr. Kallen?"

Her full smile showed perfectly shaped, white teeth. No lipstick, just gloss. It didn't look like she wore any other makeup, but she was a striking, girl-next-door kind of pretty. "If you want. Or you can call me Allie. Whatever you're comfortable with."

Allie. That fit much better than Dr. Kallen. "Oh—kay."

She pressed her lips together and looked down at their still-joined hands.

"Sorry." He let go and looked around the room. Anywhere but at her. At least until the heat faded from his cheeks. Her office wasn't what he expected either. He thought it would be something like Jacey's—modern, minimalistic. Instead, it looked like the family room from his childhood home; pale blue paint disguising the cement-block walls, overstuffed furniture, plush cream carpet. A mini fridge sat next to the couch, and a bowl of pumpkin seeds beckoned from the coffee table. "How'd you know?"

"The pumpkin seeds? I asked around. Have a seat." She gestured toward the couch and sat in the chair adjacent to it.

Reese hesitated but lowered himself onto the sofa. He didn't know what to think of her talking to others behind his back. It seemed ... manipulative. "You gonna tell me you know the name of my first dog, too?"

"Does it bother you that I did some research?"

"This whole thing bothers me."

"I know what you mean." Her voice was smooth and quiet, and it gnawed on his nerves.

"All due respect, Doc, but I seriously doubt—"

"Junior year."

"What?"

"Junior year." She turned her dark gaze on him, but her voice remained soft, her expression unreadable. "I played netminder for Stanford University's soccer team. Number one in the division. My junior year, I tore my ACL blocking a shot, and I never played on a team again."

"If that's your idea of a pep talk …"

She laughed again. A sweet, genuine sound that warmed him even though he wanted to be mad. She leaned back and crossed her legs. "No. I'm just saying I know what it's like when an injury takes away the one thing you care about the most. It's why I went into sports psychology. Helping other athletes helped me." Her gaze darted to the side then down to her notes. Interesting. Doc might have more secrets than she was owning up to.

She cleared her throat. "And your injury is different. It may take a while, but it'll heal. You'll get back out there."

"Yeah … even if I do, now it'll be prone to re-injury. It'll follow me for the rest of my career."

"It may; it may not. Lots of players get a high ankle sprain, take a few months off, and come back better than before. Not all of them re-injure it. And you're not going to let this stop you from having a career. Right?"

"This is the *playoffs*. We have a real chance this year. I worked my ass off all season, and now I don't get to play?"

She fell quiet. He'd heard about this trick. If she didn't talk, he'd have to fill the silence. Fat chance. But she didn't *stay* quiet.

"Do you know why you're here?"

He tilted his head back to count ceiling tiles. "Boss thinks you'll help me 'cope' with warming the bench."

"Actually, it's because you fought two of your teammates and put your fist through the physical therapy wall."

He groaned and slid his hands over his face. "I apologized for that. I paid for the wall. And I shouldn't have engaged with them, but they wouldn't let up, and I couldn't take it anymore. So, what, this is anger management?"

"In a way. I want to help you deal with the frustration so you don't damage any more property ... or people. Injury is part of the game. Even for goalies. I know it's not easy to accept that."

And she did know. He wanted to hold onto the idea that no one could understand, but from what she said, she knew exactly how he felt. It kind of pissed him off.

Maybe I do *need to be here.*

The rational part of his brain—the part missing since his last minutes on the ice—reminded him he shouldn't blame this woman. It wouldn't kill him to be nice to her. If things were different, if she weren't trying to autopsy his subconscious, he'd probably ask her out. As it was, it took every ounce of his self-control to stay in the room. But he had to stick with the program. "Whatever you say, Doc."

• • •

Allie watched him and made sure to keep her expression neutral. She'd seen him in pictures before, but in person he was a lot ... bigger. Not the tallest on the team, but a good half-foot taller than her five feet, six inches. And solid. They called him The Wall, and she could see why with the way he filled out a designer t-shirt and jeans. In all of his press pictures, he smiled wide, and the gleam in his whiskey brown eyes reflected his league-renowned playful personality. Not now. Now his eyes were blank, but his white-knuckled grip on the armrest said anger simmered under the surface.

Maybe he thought he was fooling her, or maybe he didn't care one way or the other. But she knew that fake complacent look. She'd worn it day in and day out for a year after her injury. Her chest felt tight. Professional distance was sometimes easier said than done. "Do you think you need to be here?"

He stared at the wall, lifted a shoulder.

Well, that was a big, fat no. "Shane—"

"Reese. Everybody calls me Reese. Even my parents."

"Reese. It's all right if you're angry. I'd be more concerned if you weren't. But it's important to work through it so you don't climb out of your skin while your ankle heals."

"Little late for that, or I wouldn't be here, right?"

Ah, there it was—some shame in his voice and a touch of humility. A good place to start. "Punching the wall was a moment of frustration. Everyone has them. And I'm willing to bet Collier and Scott weren't innocent angels supporting you from the sidelines."

He smirked.

"Right. I'm not condoning what you did to them; I'm just saying I know you were provoked."

"I was. But that's no excuse."

The last part sounded robotic, like a quote from his coach, Nealy Windham—something he'd had to write on a mental chalkboard a hundred times. It had her fabled corporal punishment ring to it. "You have a right to feel whatever you're feeling. Then, now, always. Just channel your reaction. You feel like taking down a teammate, hit the heavy bag instead."

He nodded. He may have heard it before, but he needed to keep hearing it until it sunk in. Still, that sheen of anger in his eyes remained. He wasn't just having a hard time sitting out. There was something else.

His pocket buzzed. He fished out a cell phone and hit a button. "Sorry. I have physical therapy at ten."

"It's all right. I think we're done for today anyway."

"Today …?"

"You didn't think this was a one-shot deal, did you?"

The look of abject shock said he did. Allie bit back a smile. "Sorry. You're stuck with me until you're back on the ice. Tuesdays and Thursdays."

His jaw tightened, and his fingers twitched before he stood. "I guess I'll see you Thursday then."

"See you Thursday."

Allie took in the tense set of his shoulders as he left, and she held her breath. Five seconds later, the crack of a hand slapping cinderblock echoed through the hall. At least the basement walls weren't plaster. She leaned back in the armchair and studied the ceiling. Shane Reese did not hide his feelings well, but that was good news. There might be hope for him yet.

Chapter Two

Reese pulled into his driveway and sat there for a minute. Another day not on the ice. Another day of physical therapy. It was almost a punishment in itself, forced to go through the motions of "getting better" when nothing got better. A high ankle sprain was a slippery injury. Other players all had different recovery stories. None of it helped him. He turned up the radio. Just when his blood pressure approached normal, his phone went off, and he jumped.

His mom. Second time she'd called that morning.

Ignore.

As much as he loved her, he did *not* feel like talking. And oh, would she want to talk. He just didn't have it in him to hear about church bingo; the neighbor's dog; whatever crazy, new thing his baby sister had done; or, worst of all, how *he* was doing.

He switched the car off, swung his legs out of the Explorer, and eased onto his good, right foot before putting pressure on the air cast encasing his left. Just a twinge of discomfort, but that could be misleading. Walk a little too fast, lean a little too much, and fire would flame from his ankle up his calf. Some days it would start out feeling good as new. Then, just as recovery seemed tangible, the pain would come back, mocking him. *Everyone who thinks life is looking up, take a step forward. Not so fast, Reese.*

He locked the car and hobbled the short trip to his front door. As he put the key in the lock, the knob turned in his hand without any resistance. His heart beat hard, and his skin went cold even under the Vegas sun as the door swung open. He locked it every day. Forgetting wasn't even an option. For someone as superstitious as a goalie, habits were so ingrained, they took no thought.

"Hello?"

No answer. Not that he expected one. What was a thief going to say? *"Yeah, I'm in the kitchen, making a sandwich. Want one?"* Reese reached to the right and grabbed his goalie stick leaning against the coat rack. It wouldn't be much protection against a gun, but he could wield it well enough to keep a knife away. The term *blocking shots* popped in his head, and he smiled despite the unease clawing at his chest.

The living room to the immediate left was empty, and the kitchen straight ahead appeared clear too. He dug his cell phone out of his pocket with one hand as he inched forward. Before he could thumb-dial 911, a whirling woman danced into view, long, light brown hair bouncing as she spun in circles around the kitchen island. He took a step back; heart slamming hard in his chest, then released a deep breath as he saw her face.

"Dammit, Saralynn."

She kept dancing; the wire from her ear buds cluing him in to her oblivion. As she spotted a turn, he waved his stick and she shrieked, stumbling to a stop. She pulled out the ear buds, and a muted version of her pop music filled the silence.

"Jeez, Reese. Give a girl a little warning. Do you greet your dates that way? 'Cause I could see how that'd prevent a girlfriend."

"Are you kidding me? Seriously?"

"What?" She stood hands on hips, head cocked. Her acid-wash denim shorts were too short, and her tank top exposed her belly button. Their mother would have a heart attack. Saralynn might be twenty-one, but with an eight-year age difference, she'd always be his baby sister.

"What are you doing here?"

"Um, crashing. Remember?" She picked a grape from the bowl on the island and popped it in her mouth.

His blood pressure crept back up. "What are you talking about?"

"Mom said she told you. I called you, too. Since when don't you answer your phone?"

Since his injury became all anyone wanted to talk about.

He held up his cell and unlocked the screen, stared at the voicemail icon, and clenched his jaw. "I've been busy."

"Busy moping, you mean?"

"Saralynn …"

"Okay, sorry. Withdrawn." But her smile didn't look sorry. "All right, if you haven't checked your messages, guess I have to catch you up." She hopped to sit on the island and swung her legs back and forth. "I need to crash here a while. I heard there were some job opportunities in Vegas, and Mom thought it'd be a good idea to stay with you until I settle in. Do you mind?"

Then she hit him with it. The doe-eyed stare, child-like smile, and slumped shouldered trio no one could resist. He'd had a lifetime of practice trying, but when she looked at him like that, protective, big brother came to the forefront and put his pride in check. Somehow, she was no longer Saralynn at twenty-one. She was Saralynn at eight. And he was screwed.

"You can stay. But a few months tops, okay? This might not be the best city for you. It's big and dangerous, Sare."

"You sound like Mom." She stuck her tongue out at him.

He sighed. "Yeah, I don't say this often, but Ma's right. Vegas isn't nice to pretty, young girls."

"I'm not a *girl* anymore, Grandpa. I can take care of myself."

Clearly. That's why their mother signed him up to babysit.

"You *are* a girl, and you *will* be careful. What kind of job are you looking for anyway?" He limped back to the front door to close it and replace his stick against the hat rack. When he got back to the kitchen, his sister had moved on from the grapes to eat one of his apples. The girl could eat like a hockey player and not gain an ounce. His food budget would double.

"I was hoping to get a PR internship somewhere. Maybe … with your team?"

"Uh, I don't think that's a good idea, Sare." She shouldn't be anywhere near his teammates. She'd flirt, the guys would respond, he'd have to kick the shit out of them—again—and then he'd never get out of therapy.

"C'mon, please? What could it hurt? It's a reputable organization. A safe place to work. I don't even expect a salary. I'm just out of college. I have to build my work experience before I can get *the* job. This would be a steppingstone. I'm not saying you have to vouch for me, just tell me who to talk to."

He could feel the vein in his forehead throbbing and rubbed it, trying to will away a stroke. He did *not* need this right now … his little sister hanging around his arena, representing his team in public. Not that Saralynn wasn't capable. As far as he'd known, she'd done well in school. She was just a little … flaky. He could picture her selling paintings barefoot on Venice Beach better than he could see her in a respectable suit selling the Sinners to the media.

Still, alternatives flashed through his mind. Saralynn waiting tables in a casino. Saralynn serving drinks behind a wild bar. Saralynn as a showgirl. "Fine. I'll ask around and let you know."

"Thank you, thank you, thank you!" She jumped off the counter and hugged him, rocking him back a step. His chin fit on top of her head like it always had, and warmth spread in his chest. The weeks of isolation hit him, and for a second, it just felt good to be with family. Pushing everyone away hadn't been a conscious decision, just a reflex. Something he hadn't realized even though people had accused him of it again and again.

"Sure. So, guest room's upstairs, first door on the right."

"Oh, yeah, I already found it. I was going to take yours because of the balcony, but I saw your clothes in the closet. Only way I could tell someone actually lived there. Where's all your stuff?"

"I don't have a lot of stuff. I'm not here much. We do a lot of road games."

"Ahh. Hey. When can I meet your team?" Mischief gleamed in her eyes, and that little-kid smile turned coy.

"Hah, yeah, never. No way."

"Oh, come—"

"Nope. Not if I can help it. I guess if you get the job, there might be some PR event that could involve a handshake, but that's it. I mean it, Saralynn. I have to live with those guys."

She pursed her lips and narrowed her eyes. "Okay, fine." The fight was not over. This might appear like a concession, but he knew her better than that. He could see the gears still turning. Fantastic. A bright smile took over, and she flipped her hair behind her. "How 'bout pizza for dinner?"

Finally, one request he didn't have a problem with.

• • •

Allie sat straight in the chair behind her desk, watching the seconds tick by on the wall clock. Five minutes until the end of her office hours, and not a single player had come in all day. She'd even propped her door open to be more welcoming. Hard to say why she had expected differently, but Reese's first session should have tipped her off. She was a pariah. And any guy who dared step foot in her office would be equally ostracized.

A little spark of anxiety flickered in her chest. How could she prove herself as a therapist if she didn't have patients? Sure, there was Reese, but one potential success didn't rebuild a reputation.

Movement in the hall caught her eye, and she bolted out of her chair and around the desk before the motive even crystallized in her brain. "Hey!"

As she got to her doorway, the man stopped and looked over his shoulder. He may not be on the team anymore, but everything about Carter Phlynn still said hockey player from his lumbering gait to his face-off expression. His features softened slightly when he saw her, and a polite smile curled the edge of his mouth. "Oh, hi. You must be the new ... doc. Kallen, right?"

That hesitation before "doc" most likely meant he'd scrolled through a few other terms first. Shrink, witch doctor, voodoo priestess ...

"Yeah. Yes. It's, uh, nice to meet you. I'm sorry to bother, but do you have a minute?"

Carter appeared to wage an inner debate, probably, like everyone else; weighing what being seen with her would do to his street cred. He shrugged and stuffed his hands in his pockets. "Sure. What's up?"

She backed up a step and gestured him into her office. He stood at the threshold and leaned a shoulder against the doorway. Apparently, that was as far as he was willing to go.

"I was talking to your wife yesterday, and she mentioned ..." Allie glanced up and down the empty hallway and lowered her voice. "She said you're thinking about trading Reese in the off-season."

His face closed down.

Damn it.

"I'm not looking for gossip, I just need to fully understand the situation if I'm going to help him through his injury. I need all the puzzle pieces. I take it he knows?"

Carter stayed quiet, and it was hard to tell what he was thinking. Good game face. Finally, he stood straight and folded his arms. "He probably does. That kind of word gets around sometimes. It's not a set decision. And it's not just about his injury. He may think that, but it's not. His play hasn't been up to par for a while."

Now, it started to make sense.

"Okay. Thanks. Jacey was just filling me in. She cares a lot about this team on a personal level. It's nice to see in an owner and a good quality in a boss."

Carter's hard mask cracked bit by bit, his jaw muscles not quite as tight. "Yeah. The team's lucky to have her. So am I."

Allie nodded. She didn't want to push her luck, but Mr. Enigma definitely had walls up, and the therapist in her had to try. "So, how's retirement treating you?"

The question took him off-guard judging by the slight flinch at the corners of his eyes, but he squeezed out a lackluster smile. "Great. Great. I mean, it's not like I'm sitting at home collecting stamps," he said with a strained laugh.

Right. But it wasn't like he was back out on the ice, either.

She smiled to let him save face. "That's true. So you're enjoying the other side of the business?"

Vulnerability and raw truth flickered in his eyes, and for a second, she thought he might actually come clean. She knew the urge was there. Pretending to be fine was an injured athlete's mainstay. It kept them from falling apart. She could absolutely attest to that. But inside them all was the desperate need to tell someone—just one person—that they weren't okay. That's why she did what she did. Why she waitressed through grad school and lived on peanut butter and jelly and grilled cheese through the last half of her twenties. So she could be that person.

Carter's walls went up again, and he nodded. "You know, it's different, but I like it. It's a new challenge."

That much was probably true. And that was all she'd get from him for now. "Well, I'm glad to hear it. I'll let you go. I didn't mean to take up a lot of your time. I just want to say I'm really happy to be here, and I look forward to making a positive difference with this team."

Skepticism mixed with the kindness in his eyes, but he finally gave her a genuine smile. "Well, we're happy to have you. And

I appreciate you trying to help Reese. I heard you were a soccer goalie?"

She nodded.

"Then you understand. Any athlete's game is ninety percent mental, but especially a goalie's. If anyone can get him back on track, I'm sure it's you."

Her face flooded with warmth, and she willed away the red that had to be in her cheeks. He didn't really know her, couldn't know how much that comment meant. It'd been a long time since she'd had that kind of faith in herself. She cleared her throat and smiled. "Thank you."

"Sure. See you around."

When he disappeared down the hallway, she closed her eyes and dropped onto the couch usually reserved for her patients. It was super soft, and she sank into the cushions, leaning her head back. At least she'd refrained from begging him to require the rest of the team to visit her. But that was okay. All athletes had issues. From what she'd learned the hard way, hockey players most of all. It was only a matter of time.

At least for the moment, the mystery of Shane Reese was starting to clear. If he'd been off his game before the injury and knew he might get traded, that explained a lot of his rage. Carter was right. Reese might want to blame the potential trade on his injury, but he didn't strike her as stupid or delusional. On some level, he probably thought he deserved it. On the surface, however, it was easier to blame someone else.

And that explained some of Carter's walls. It couldn't be easy to go from playing on the ice with your best friend to suddenly being in the position to trade him.

A light knock on the door brought her back to the moment, and she pushed to her feet then straightened her blouse.

A younger guy stood in her doorway wearing a Sinners t-shirt, Bermuda shorts, and a shy smile. "Uh, hi. Didn't mean to scare you. I'm Dylan Cole. I just finished up a workout. Heading home and I saw your door open. Thought I could walk you to your car. With the underground garage, you just want to be safe."

The unexpected kindness made her smile. "That'd be great. Thanks. Just let me get my stuff." It was easy enough to collect. She pulled the blazer from the back of her desk chair and slid it on, then scooped up her purse and messenger bag and followed him out, locking the door behind her.

"So you're Dr. Kallen." Dylan walked beside her, keeping an eye out as they entered the garage.

It sounded so formal. They were already afraid of her. "Allie's fine."

"Allie Kallen. Anyone ever call you Kally?"

She laughed. "Not since I left the field in college."

"Field … hockey?"

"Soccer."

"Pretty close. That's cool. You understand our game then." He grinned, and hope sprouted in her chest.

Maybe they'd come around sooner rather than later. "I believe I do. This is me, here." She stopped beside her red Camry and beeped it unlocked. "Thanks for walking me."

"Hey, no problem. Welcome to the Sinners. See you around, Kally." He winked over his shoulder as he headed for his own car. Day two, and she had a nickname. Things were looking up after all.

Chapter Three

Thursday, April 18th

Normally, going in early was a pain in the ass, but not today. After being blasted awake by Saralynn's *morning music*, Reese couldn't escape the house fast enough. It even made what he was about to do a little more palatable. His sister needed to get out. ASAP. This was his best shot. He said a silent prayer and knocked on Jacey's office door.

"Come in."

He eased inside and found her leafing through a stack of papers on her desk. When she saw him, her warm smile brought his guilt to the surface, but he didn't ask for favors every day. And the war at home meant desperate measures. "Hey, Boss. Got a sec?"

"Reese, you were the best man at my wedding. I think you can call me Jacey. And sure, what's up?"

He tried to swallow, but his throat clicked. "Well, my sister, Saralynn, just moved here, and she's looking for work. She has a degree in public relations, and she just wants an internship. I told her I'd ask if there was anything open." There. He said it. Equal parts hope and trepidation built up in his chest. If Saralynn got the job, she'd be out of the house during the day at least. She'd also be in his arena. Hard to pick the lesser of the two evils.

Jacey's face lit up, and she held up one finger then shuffled through some flyers. "Actually, yeah. I think an internship did just open up. We always look for more help around playoffs. We try to have more of a PR presence at the games handing out free swag, helping fans sign up for text alerts and all that." She plucked a neon green piece of paper from the bunch and held it out to him.

21

It was odd to feel relief and anxiety at the same time. He skimmed the flyer and nodded. "Thanks. I'll pass this along to her."

"It is an internship like you said, so it's unpaid, but if we like her work, we might take her on full time. It happens, but don't get her hopes up just yet."

"Oh no, I totally understand. She would be happy to get the experience. Thanks a lot. Really."

Jacey grinned and quirked a brow. "She's getting to you, huh? How long has it been?"

Heat crept up his neck and he studied the carpet, unable to fight back a smile. "Uh ... a day."

She laughed, and it eased some of his tension. It had felt weird talking to her after he heard about his potential trade. Not as weird as talking to Carter, but it was definitely far from the easy comfort level they'd found after last year's Cup win. Jacey had become family when she married his best friend. Then things got complicated when the business of the game cut in.

She seemed on the verge of saying something but must have decided against it. Instead, she softened her smile, and the pity in her eyes made his stomach go sour. "Good news is, if Saralynn gets the job, she'll be too busy to drive you crazy. How do you like Dr. Kallen?"

He took a step backward and reached for the door. "Great. She's fine. She's ... different."

"Not what you expected, huh? Do me a favor, and just give her a chance."

"Sure. Thanks again for this." He held up the flyer and edged out of her office. "See you later, Boss." Didn't feel right calling her Jacey. Not if he might have to put this team and maybe his best friend behind him. Before she could reply, he closed the door and headed for the elevator. Time for physical therapy and then round two with the head shrinker.

• • •

Allie leaned back in her desk chair and tapped the tip of a pen against the notepad in her lap. Randomly at first, and then a song popped into her head, so she matched the imaginary drumbeat. An hour until her next session with Shane. *Reese*. Whatever. Most athletes were used to being called by their last names or nicknames, but Shane's comment that even his parents called him Reese threw her a bit. She could imagine him as a little boy, embracing his goalie role so much he wanted his family to call him the same thing his teammates did. One personality on and off the ice. Not so common, but interesting.

Hmm. She checked her notes. Thursdays he had physical therapy before their session. Couldn't hurt to see. His physical progress affected his mental progress. She pushed out of her chair, keys in hand, and locked the office behind her. A short stroll down the hall, and she stopped in front of the window exposing the PT room. Normally, there'd be three or four players working with various machines and trainers, but today it was just Reese. Probably a good call as volatile as he'd been.

Bill, the head trainer, had Reese sitting on the ground, legs stretched out straight. He rotated Reese's bad ankle while the goalie sucked air through his teeth. Reese wore nothing but board shorts, and there were still a few water droplets on his back, so hydrotherapy must be done for the day. One particular twist had Reese slamming the ground with his fist, and Bill eased off.

Allie pursed her lips and sighed. Just as she backed away, Reese tucked his good foot under him and stood, balancing without a waver while Bill put the air cast back on. She returned to her office and fell into her chair, rubbing her face. A challenging patient was nothing new. A challenging patient with anger issues equaled a guaranteed pain in the ass *and* a longer recovery.

She straightened her posture and adjusted her blazer just before Reese walked in. To the board shorts, he'd added a long-sleeved, Sinners t-shirt, socks rolled up to his knees, and one Adidas slip-on sandal opposite his cast. His hair stood out in wet, dark brown spikes, and he ran a hand through them as he dropped onto the couch. "What's up, Doc?" No smile but no animosity either. He tipped his head back and yawned wide.

"The usual. You missing some sleep?" She moved to the armchair that faced the couch and sat, crossing her legs. His gaze tracked the motion but only for a nanosecond before he closed his eyes.

"Yeah, but it's not my fault. My sister's staying with me until she can find a job and a place. She rises with the sun like a rooster, and when Saralynn is awake, she makes sure nobody can sleep."

Interesting how he assumed she was accusing him. "That's got to be stressful."

"Add it to the list. Oh, and she wants a job here."

"Here?"

"With the Sinners. PR internship."

"How do you feel about that?"

He cracked an eye open and hesitated.

• • •

There was that question again. Why did women always want to know how he *felt*? His mom. Saralynn. Jacey. Well okay, Allie had pretty straightforward motives. It was her job. *Do me a favor and just give her a chance.* Jacey's words echoed and compelled him to answer against his better judgment. "I guess this is one of the better places my sister could work in Vegas."

"It can be tough; family working together."

"Well, I wouldn't actually be working *with* her. Contact would be minimal most days. We'd only cross paths at public events. Signings, meet-and-greets; that kinda thing."

"Are you going to introduce her to the team?"

A short laugh burst out like a gunshot, and he shook his head. "Uh, no. I love those guys like brothers. I'd like to avoid the mess."

The smallest smile flickered at Allie's glossed lips. "You don't trust them with her?"

"I don't trust *her* with *them*. Saralynn has a habit of wrapping men around her finger until she gets bored and moves on. Fine for her, but there's no moving on for me." *Unless I'm traded.* That thought showed up more and more often and made his heart sink. As much as he loved this team and the people behind it, he was expendable. In his eleven-year professional career the nature of the business had never bothered him. Trades were a part of life. A horrible part, but unavoidable in hockey. And he'd always been traded with Phlynn before. For the first time, he might have to move on his own.

"You're quiet. What are you thinking about?"

Reese glanced up and found her watching him. He crossed his arms and lifted a shoulder. "Just ... what I'm going to do with my sister. She *is* driving me crazy." If a diversion were true, it didn't count as a lie, right?

Allie narrowed her eyes slightly and smiled in a way that tightened his gut. Apparently her bullshit meter was pretty fine-tuned. Great. Every minute he spent with her, odds seemed worse he'd be able to fake his way to a clean bill of mental health. Time to switch tactics.

"How 'bout we talk about physical therapy and how it doesn't seem to be working?"

She hesitated, and he knew he had her. No doubt her shrink instincts told her to pursue his silence, but no way could she pass up something as valid as his PT woes. Allie carefully folded her hands on her knee. "I know it's frustrating. The trainers are doing everything they should. This is just a tricky injury."

"Yeah, well another month of this, and I'll cut my foot off and skate with a prosthesis."

"I remember that feeling. I wanted to cleave my leg off above the knee rehabbing from the ACL surgery."

He fought a grin and lost. "What held you back?"

"Couldn't give these up." She lifted the crossed leg to show off a sexy shoe with a four-inch heel.

Her intention probably wasn't to turn him on, but he had to look away and readjust his sitting position. "I don't have that problem."

"No, but you also couldn't balance in goalie skates with a prosthetic, and as frustrating as it gets, I'll bet that'll hold you back."

He pressed his lips together and appraised her. Here he was, clinging to irrational, last-ditch solutions, and she couldn't even let him have that.

"You *will* recover from this. You know how you can't hurry love? You also can't hurry a high ankle sprain. It was originally in the song, but they cut it because nothing rhymes with ankle. It'll heal in its own time."

"What if I don't *have* time?"

A light went on in her brown eyes.

Shit. How could he slip? Did she have a voodoo doll under her desk?

"Do you want to talk about the trade rumors?" She knew, then. Figured.

"Rumors, threats; whatever."

"Reese, it's not a threat. You've been in this game a long time. You know how it works." Her soft, even tone didn't make it any easier to swallow.

"Okay, ultimatum then. And you can't tell me that's not what it is. I improve or I move. Bottom line."

She licked her lips. It would have been distracting if she didn't already have his guard up. "Do you think it's harder this time because of who would be moving you?"

Low blow. But that was the point, wasn't it? Her job was to crack him open like one of the pumpkin seeds she used to buy his cooperation. Well, good luck with that. Sure, it hurt that his best friend didn't have enough faith in his ability to keep him on after twenty-five years of playing together. Nothing had changed except Phlynn's new place of power. He seemed pretty fond of that throne he was sitting on.

"No. A trade is a trade. But it's not my fault I got injured. I'd give anything to be out there, defending my team."

She nodded but fell quiet. The silence stretched, and he was ready to break through the concrete wall to escape when his phone buzzed in his pocket. Session over. Thank God.

He stood. "Good talk, but looks like time's up. Guess I'll see you Tuesday."

She looked disappointed. While it should have annoyed him, he felt a stab of guilt for putting that expression on her pretty face. Definitely time to go.

"Sure. See you Tuesday."

He put every ounce of effort into walking with the least limp possible, shutting her door behind him. Once free, he closed his eyes and begged for strength. How would he survive another week, let alone a potential month, of sessions with Doctor Feelings?

Chapter Four

Friday, April 19th

Allie grabbed her keys off the kitchen table, slung her messenger bag over her shoulder, and locked up. The neighborhood reminded her of home back in Pennsylvania. The houses were modest, traditional, and didn't have flashing, neon lights. Seeing her buttercup yellow siding every day lessened the feeling of living in adult Disneyland.

The world transformed on her drive into work from Pleasant Valley Sunday to Viva Las Vegas. Monster buildings lined the streets and somehow still sparkled just as much in the early morning sun as they did in the middle of the night. She swung into the arena lot and parked in the underground garage. The basement hallway was empty as usual, but the yelling and whistle blowing of hockey practice echoed faintly. Home sweet home.

Her office felt like a mausoleum, stagnant and silent. Enough of that. She deposited her stuff behind her desk and turned on the MP3 player in its docking station. For patients, she sometimes used nature sounds or classical music. Because she only had one patient, and he wouldn't be back until Tuesday, she put on her pop mix. If she had to sit around all day and stare at the walls, *she'd* need therapy.

Audio sunshine filled the room, and she bopped around, careful of the furniture. How embarrassing would it be if a player walked in? Not much room to groove in the small space, but it still felt good to let go and allow the happy, infectious beat to flow through her. She was mid spin when a quiet knock eased the door open. Allie froze as her stomach dropped somewhere in the vicinity of her feet.

She relaxed and laughed as she took in the timid woman staring at her instead of a hulking hockey player. Allie turned off the music and finger-combed her hair. "Sorry about that. I wasn't expecting anyone."

"Oh no, it's my fault. I should have called first or something, but I didn't have your number. I don't know if this is actually okay. I mean, I'm not on the *team* team, but I am on the dance team. I'm not sure if your door's open to us too, but I thought I'd check. I'm Miranda."

Miranda huddled against the doorframe in a Lady Sinners glittery tank top, yoga pants, and athletic sneakers. Her long, dark hair was pulled back in a smooth ponytail, and while she didn't wear eye shadow, fake lashes outlined her light eyes, and her lips were glossed to pink perfection. Las Vegas. Women dolled up just to work out.

Allie paused. No one had mentioned if the dancers could make appointments. Probably not since they weren't technically part of the team, but the actual team didn't want to see her. And Miranda, smiling politely at the floor and shifting uncomfortably, clearly needed to.

"Come on in. My morning's open." So was the rest of her day, but no need to announce that. Allie grabbed her notepad and a pen from her desk, flipped to a clean sheet, and sat in the armchair.

Miranda closed the door behind her, sat carefully on the edge of the couch, and promptly burst into tears. She held her face with her elbows on her knees and hiccupped through her sobs.

It wasn't a total surprise. The dancer's body language and hesitancy broadcasted a fragile girl, but Allie still felt a ping of anxiety at how suddenly the dam burst. She picked the box of tissues off her desk and handed them to her.

Miranda sniffled and dabbed at her face then blew her nose. "I'm really sorry."

"It's okay. You don't have to apologize." Allie fell quiet while the other woman composed herself. Best to let her explain when she was ready. Unlike Reese, Miranda seemed desperate to unload. It was a nice change of pace. Maybe she'd actually make a difference today.

"My boyfriend ..." Her voice broke, and she sniffed. "He uh ... broke up with me last week. I really loved him, but it's probably for the best. He wasn't always the nicest guy."

That explained all the apologizing. Manipulative people had a way of turning things around to make the victims feel guilty. It seemed so ingrained in Miranda that she apologized to everybody. Allie kept her expression blank and tried to leave her own emotion out even though she'd like to have a few words with Boyfriend. "The fact you can even tell me that proves you're right. I'm sure you are better off without him. It's normal, though, if you miss him."

"I guess I sort of do. But mostly it's that he took Baby." The last sentence ended with another sob, and she cried into her crumpled tissues.

Allie frowned and leaned forward to touch Miranda's arm lightly. "He took your child?"

"N-no." Hiccup. "Baby is my Chihuahua. We got him together, and Steven took him when he left. I called, but he won't give him back."

Allie's tension eased a notch. Not as dire, but still heartbreaking. And potentially more complicated. "Did you purchase Baby together?"

Miranda's lips quivered before she pursed them hard. "Steven bought him, but as a gift for me. I paid for the food and the vet bills."

"Talk to a lawyer. You might be able to take legal action to get Baby back. It's worth a try."

"You think so?"

"I think it could be your best bet. I wouldn't advise confronting Steven on your own."

Thoughtful if wary hope replaced the despair on Miranda's face, and the corner of her mouth twitched in a small smile. "Thank you. Dr. Kallen, right?"

"Right, but you can call me Allie. I'm not sure if it's covered in your contract, but if you need to talk and I'm not in a session, you're welcome here. The other Lady Sinners, too. My doctorate is in sports psychology, but real life affects sports performance, so anything goes." Management might not be happy, but she should do *something* to earn her salary. And if no one ever came in her office except Reese, who would know?

"Thank you so much. Really. And I'm sorry again for just showing up and falling apart."

"Miranda, you don't need to apologize. Really." Allie smiled and stood.

The dancer followed suit. "Hey, I don't mean to embarrass you, but you had some good moves when I walked in. You should come practice with us Monday night. The girls would love to have you, and I think you'd have fun."

"Oh, I don't know …"

"Come on. You'll love it. Just one practice."

Unexpected excitement tempered the urge to decline. The only teams she'd been a part of kicked soccer balls. What was she always telling patients? Venture outside your comfort zone. "Okay, I'll do it."

"Great! It's at seven on Monday night. They're designing a practice room down here for next season, but in the mean time, we rehearse on the executive level. You know the big conference room opposite the offices? The walls are all windows, and at night, they're as good as mirrors. After we get the routine, we go down to center ice, roll out the mat, and do a final run-through."

"I'll be there. Is there a dress code?"

"Whatever you wear to workout will be fine." Miranda smiled, and backed out of the office. "See you Monday."

"See you Monday." Once the door closed, Allie smiled to herself and turned the music back on. Possibly it crossed some professional boundary for the team psychologist to shake her thang with the cheerleaders, but she was at least ninety percent sure she couldn't get fired for it.

• • •

Monday, April 22nd

At seven o'clock, Allie pulled into the arena's surface lot. With the halogen lampposts, it would be bright as day when she got out and probably safer than the garage. She slung her gym bag over a shoulder and headed for the main entrance. Even though the lobby was empty, she resisted the urge to cover up. If Jacey or Carter—or worse, Reese—saw her, she might have exploded from embarrassment.

She made a beeline for the elevator and punched in the code for the executive level, flattening herself in a corner until the doors slid closed. A deep exhale relaxed her shoulders. At this time of night, the offices would be empty. Safe. The elevator pinged when it reached the top floor. As the doors slid open and heads turned in the glass-walled conference room, a new kind of anxiety bubbled in her chest. What was with the looks?

For a second, it felt like being snubbed by the high school cheerleaders, but the Lady Sinners' smiles weren't condescending. A few of them were laughing, though. Miranda bounced over and took Allie's hands with an excited giggle. "You're here! I'm so psyched. Come on and meet everybody."

Allie's smile wavered. "Sure. Uh, why are they looking at me like that?"

"Oh. We usually practice in Sinners gear and yoga pants, but your outfit is fine. And I have something that'll help." Miranda dropped one of Allie's hands but kept the other and tugged her toward the conference room. Allie skidded behind and looked down at herself. Black sports bra and soccer shorts. Socks rolled up to her knees and sneakers. Then she looked around the room. It was true. Every other woman there wore second-skin yoga pants and tight black tank tops that said Lady Sinners in glittering, white rhinestones. The "s" at the end of Sinners had a pointed devil's tail dangling down.

Miranda darted away only to return a blink later. "Hands up."

Allie complied, and Miranda slipped a matching tank top over her head. Silly, but it did help. She didn't feel like the weird outsider anymore. The other women cheered and clapped, and Allie laughed as her muscles relaxed.

"Girls, this is Allie, the one I told you about. Allie, that's Marissa, Selena, Candi, Amber, Yvonne, Cammy, Audrey, Teresa, Shelly, Bianca, Jamie, Leighanne, Sasha, and Ricky."

Lots of names, and they all looked sort of similar with the high hair and heavy makeup, but a good memory was part of her job. "It's nice to meet you all. Thanks for letting me join a practice."

"We're happy to have you, right ladies?"

The women cheered again, and when they quieted, Selena stepped forward. "Miranda said we could stop by your office if we ever need to talk about something?"

"Sure. As long as I'm not in session with a player, you're all welcome. I'm there every day nine to five, and my only booked sessions right now are Tuesdays and Thursdays at ten."

Smiles all around. Murmurs echoed for a minute before Miranda hit the play button on the stereo. "Okay, let's get started!"

It took all of twenty seconds for Allie to feel completely lost. She chose a spot in the back to avoid being the center of attention, but it happened anyway when she stumbled into … well, everyone.

Understanding a soccer play was one thing. There was a plan. It made sense. It allowed for adaptations on the fly. Dancing did not. There appeared to be a plan, but she didn't have it.

Miranda led up front, facing them and counting out the steps. Their reflections danced along in the window wall. What had Miranda said before? They practiced here until everyone got the routine, then they went down to the ice. At this rate, Allie would have them here until midnight. She edged out of line and stood back, watching everyone for a minute. Easier to get a handle on things when you weren't running over people.

With a bit of distance, it looked less random, and patterns emerged. The steps weren't as tricky as they seemed in the middle of the action. Under her breath, she counted along with Miranda and tried abbreviated versions of the moves in her little spot against the wall of glass.

When the fast-paced song ended, Miranda shouted, "Okay, from the top!" She hit play again, and this time, Allie felt ready. She hopped back in line and still counted in her head as she fell into step with the other women. Something clicked. The dance sequences lined up with the music, and before she knew it, everything made sense. No more thinking ahead. Somehow, her body knew what to do and when. It felt a lot like goaltending in an odd way, and she couldn't hold in a laugh.

The women around her whoo-hooed and yelled, "Yeah, Allie!"

Camaraderie felt good. Not just that, the *dancing* felt good. It was sexy and over-the-top, nothing she'd be comfortable with in any other scenario, but there was something freeing about it. Empowering. She had expected to feel ridiculous, maybe degraded, but it wasn't anything like that. These weren't women who needed male approval for their self-worth. They were confident, comfortable with their bodies, and brave enough to showcase that. Humbling, and for once, she was happy to be wrong.

"All *right!*" Miranda turned the music off and clapped. "Awesome, ladies! Let's take this down to the ice."

Everyone grabbed their towels and water bottles and filed out. Allie snagged her gym bag, rehydrated, and wiped the sweat from her face. While they waited for the elevator, she caught her breath. "If anyone ever says you guys aren't athletes, they don't know what they're talking about."

The women laughed and headed down in two shifts. By the time Allie's group got there, the first group had set up the large square of carpet at center ice. Her sneakers provided decent traction, but she relaxed a little more when they reached the mat. Miranda set up the stereo on the players' bench, then glided over almost as if she were on skates and took her place up front. The music came on, and Allie came alive.

• • •

Reese walked out of the showers with minimal limping, and hope rose in his chest. Stupid. It didn't mean anything. Tomorrow the pain could be back if he so much as slept wrong. Still, any improvement was better than a relapse. Much better to work on physical therapy at night. No heckling teammates or well-meaning trainers. The faster he got back, the better. The Sinners just swept the Kings in the first playoff round. Without him. When he got cleared, at best he'd be designated to back-up goaltender. At worst … He dried off and dressed on autopilot. As he pulled on his mesh shorts, he froze.

Pop music echoed and boomed from outside the locker room. He frowned. Who else would be here this late? After securing his walking cast—better safe than sorry—and slipping on the one shoe, he eased down the tunnel to the ice. The rink lights were on full blast, so he stayed in shadow. A bunch of barely dressed women jumped around to the music. The Lady Sinners. Their costumes were just as memorable as their dance moves.

They swayed their hips, shook their chests and tossed their hair to the music, but no one was watching *him*, and he couldn't look away. Maybe that made him a pig, but no straight man in his position could do differently. The group parted so one dancer could have a solo, and this girl could *move*. Fluid. Beautiful. Undeniably sexual. His heart beat faster, and arousal canceled out the cold air of the rink.

The women chanted, "Go Allie! Go Allie!"

No.

It couldn't be. There was no way. He moved a little closer and squinted. The hair color was right, and the length. Her form-fitting business clothes had given his imagination a lot to work with, and the body he saw on the ice was a close match. That skin-tight tank top crystallized the picture. The loose soccer shorts and knee-high socks didn't even take away from how hot she was. Honestly, they added a new element to the fantasy.

Just so hard to process. The straight-laced shrink could do *that*? She could *look* like that? Great. How was he supposed to sit in session with her now and not undress her in his head? How was he supposed to keep the dumbass smile off his face when she talked to him about channeling frustration?

As the song ended, the women gathered around Allie with hugs and high-fives. Shane headed back down the tunnel to the locker room, waddling and limping at the same time. He needed to cool off before he went home. And he'd have to face Saralynn. That thought was a cold shower all by itself.

Chapter Five

She had one hour until her appointment with Reese. Plenty of time. Allie turned into the Las Vegas Sports Park and found a spot in front of the Summerlin Soccer Complex. It was nearly empty at 9:00 A.M. on a Tuesday. Stepping out of her Camry, she closed her eyes to drink in the sun like a daisy. The thought of spending seven hours in her basement dungeon-office didn't motivate her to move. The thought of seeing her old friend did.

The Summerlin lobby was tiled, and with the high ceilings, the click of her heels echoed like gunshots. A familiar man behind the sign-in desk sent her a smile, and she returned it.

"Hi, you must be David. Is Mac—"

"Kally!"

Allie turned to see a petite woman emerging from the indoor field and jogging toward her in a t-shirt and soccer shorts. Red-gold hair pulled back in a ponytail at the base of her neck, and somehow, more freckles on her face. They'd only seen each other sporadically over the last seven years, but Dana MacGuire hadn't aged a day since undergrad.

"Mac!" They hugged, and Allie almost swung her friend off her feet. "It is *so* good to see you. You have no idea. I was feeling all alone here."

Mac laughed and leaned back. "Am I good, or am I good? I knew you'd get the position! I swear Las Vegas isn't as big and scary as it seems. But I'm so glad you're here! I know we talk every day, but this is so much better."

A throat cleared behind them, and Mac's eyes widened. "Oh! Right. You two haven't formally met. The handsome man behind the desk is my husband, David. David, this is Allie Kallen, but we call her Kally."

David grinned and nodded. "It's nice to meet you. My wife's told me so much about you."

"She's told me all about you, too. I'm so sorry I couldn't be at the wedding. If I wasn't defending my thesis, I'd have done anything to make it. Listen, I'm heading into work, but I wanted to stop by and say hi. Maybe we can meet up later?" Allie bumped elbows with Mac.

"I teach clinics until nine tonight, but part of the indoor field is open after seven. If you feel like kicking around, you'd have the place to yourself. And then maybe we could do dinner tomorrow?"

"That sounds incredible. I haven't been on a field in years, but I've been dying to get back. I dream about doing drills. Is that sad?"

"Yes. But we will get into that and everything else over dinner." Mac winked. "Have you been to Culinary Dropout? It's in the Hard Rock. Good food, lot of variety, and decent prices."

"I haven't, but that sounds awesome."

"Great. How about you meet me here when you get off work, and I'll drive? David has to coach on Wednesdays, so it's a perfect girls night."

"Sounds good."

"All right, hon." Mac pulled Allie into another hug. "I can't wait to hear all about your exciting life with the Sinners. You haven't filled me in since you've been here."

"I know, I'm sorry. Things have been crazy, but I swear I'll catch you up. Okay, I'll see you later, M—I'm still calling you Mac even though you're a Sickavish now." Allie glanced over her shoulder. "Sorry, David."

"It's okay. Sometimes I still call her Mac."

Allie laughed and waved to them both as she backed through the front door. She smiled to herself all the way to her car. A tense knot she hadn't even been aware of eased in her chest. The little piece of home made the city less daunting. Then she remembered her ten o'clock appointment.

· · ·

Reese walked down the hallway from the locker room to Allie's office without limping. No cast either. An evil voice in his head whispered that it couldn't last; the pain would come back. Except it didn't, so he pushed the voice down and buried it under his resolve to get back on the ice. He braced himself to see the wanton woman from last night, but the doorknob wouldn't turn. Locked. He frowned and checked the time on his phone. A few minutes before ten, but she'd always been there early. In fact, she'd always been there, period. He was starting to think she had a sleeping bag behind her desk. Maybe she wasn't coming today. Guilt lanced him in the gut for hoping she might be sick.

Before the internal debate could wage any further, the door to the parking garage opened, and Allie jogged to meet him, key ring jingling in her hand. "Sorry I'm ..." She glanced at her wristwatch and wrinkled her nose. "You're early."

He smirked. "You say that like it never happens. I can come back in five minutes if you—"

"No, no. Let's go." She moved in close to unlock the door, and her light, fresh perfume hit him hard. Citrus and vanilla. God help him; she smelled like a Creamsicle. And in those form-fitting black pants, it was just about impossible to forget her dancing last night.

He focused on his feet and closed his eyes as soon as he dropped onto her couch. "So ... late night?" The room went silent—no more rustling from behind her desk, so he cracked an eye open.

Allie froze, staring at him blankly like someone pushed her pause button. "Um, no. I got an email this morning from a college friend. She's living in Vegas now, too, so I stopped to see her on my way in."

Too easy to push. More fun to draw it out.

"So." She busted out the pen and paper and settled in the chair facing him. "You're out of the cast. How's it feel?" Her right leg slid over the left.

The corner of his mouth twitched, and he focused instead on the vase of white flowers on the coffee table. "Good. No pain today. I did some stretches last night in the PT room. Really made a difference."

Her lack of expression was her biggest tell. After spending even this small amount of time with Allie, he knew no response meant she was thinking. Putting together that he'd been just down the hall while she was letting it all hang out. The hesitation lasted only a few seconds. "That's great. Sometimes working at your own pace is more productive. Just don't push too hard too fast."

Yadda, yadda. Bill had been chirping that at him for weeks. His glazed expression must have clued her in.

"You've heard it before. All right, let's change tacks. You're feeling better physically. Do you still want to Hulk smash your teammates?"

He sighed and leaned his head back. "I never wanted to fight them. They're like my brothers. They weren't being serious assholes, just … doing what they do. I don't know what it's like with women's teams, but guys provoke and prank relentlessly. As a sign of affection. I took it personally, and that's on me."

"We prank. Provoke other teams but not really each other. Have you told Collier and Scott you take responsibility?"

He squeezed his eyes closed and scrubbed a hand across his forehead. "We haven't really talked much."

"Maybe that's why." She twirled the pen between her fingers and stared at him with that calm, assessing, gaze.

He flashed back to the previous night, saw her bend forward, then toss her hair back in that tiny tank top. He swallowed and shifted on the couch. "Yeah."

"If you apologized, they might actually support you. Getting rid of that tension could put you in a better mindset to train, too. Get you back on the ice sooner."

"If you want me and the guys to have a Dr. Phil moment—"

"I *want* things to get back to normal for you. I really think it'll make a difference in returning you to play faster. And that's best for everybody."

He cocked an eyebrow and smirked. "Gettin' tired of me, Kally?"

She paused at his use of the nickname, but a twitch at the corner of her mouth said she wasn't really mad. "At least you're still talking to Cole. And no, I'm not tired of you. But it's my job to make sure you're ready to go back. This is an important step."

"All right. I'll talk to them. And it's not just Cole. He started it, but they all call you Kally now."

"Well, I guess that's better than 'voodoo priestess.'" She smiled, and it chipped away at his urge to antagonize her.

"That's what happens when word gets out you have everyone's favorite snack in here. They might be warming up to you."

"Not you though, right?" The teasing glint in her dark brown eyes made his cheeks burn.

He shrugged casually, tilted his head. "I guess you're okay."

"Gee, thanks." Her smile softened. That was usually a warning sign. "Can I ask you something?"

His gut tightened, and his heart beat a little faster. In his years of experience, it was never a good thing when a woman said that. Trick question ahead. "I don't think I have a choice."

"Why do you think you got injured?"

Of all the things he expected, that one didn't make the list. "Uh ... a three hundred pound Russian fell on me?"

"I know how it sounds, but my therapist asked me the same question when I tore my ACL. My answer was like yours. I dove to make a save, twisted my knee."

"I feel like I'm missing something ..."

"Our answers explained *how* we got hurt. Not why. I didn't have to dive to make that save. I could have shuffled to the left and still blocked it. It took me a while to admit the real reason. It was a championship game. The clock was ticking down. The crowd was on their feet screaming so loud I couldn't hear myself think. I wanted a really impressive save for the win."

• • •

Blank stare. Allie almost waved a hand in front of his face. He looked like a robot that had powered down. She'd expected some kind of reaction. A sympathetic smile. Even some ribbing or at least outright denial that he could have done something like that. No reaction was bad. She held in a sigh and flipped her notepad closed.

Reese looked at his phone and seemed surprised. She'd had some kind of impact at least because this was the first time he hadn't anticipated the end of a session. Apparently snapping out of wherever he'd been, he smirked, fixed her with that whiskey gaze, and made her feel like a cornered deer. "So, any fun plans after work? Maybe going dancing?"

Her heart tripped. He knew. He had to know. He'd been toying with her all session. She smiled evenly, set the pen and pad on her desk. "You saw me last night."

Those eyes lit up, and he failed at an attempt to hold back a grin. "You got some moves. Didn't peg you for a cheerleader."

"They're a *dance team*. And no, I've never shaken any pom poms."

"You sure did from where I was standing."

She resisted the urge to crawl under her desk and managed to maintain composure. "Hey, a little professional respect, please."

"I respect the hell out of you. And—"

"If you finish that sentence with 'your pom poms,' I'll break your other ankle."

The shock on his face gave way to laughter. Genuine belly laughs that made it impossible to stay mad. In all the time they'd spent together, he'd been so serious. He transformed when he was completely at ease and happy. His already handsome features took on a new light. It was almost like meeting him again for the first time. Flirting was off limits. She couldn't allow it. And yet … it was hard to deny that spark between them. *Bad therapist. Bad.*

"You know, technically, we're off the clock."

She needed cold water and lots of it. Like Niagara Falls. But, no. They lived in the desert. Even in the basement of a hockey arena, it was hard to escape the heat in her office. "There is no 'off the clock' with you."

He winced and clapped a hand over his heart. "You wound me, Kally." When she rolled her eyes, he laughed. "Seriously. I'm just curious. What do you do after work? When you're *not* auditioning for the Lady Sinners?"

Just because he baited her didn't mean she had to bite. "I wasn't auditioning. I ran into one of the dancers last week, and she invited me to a practice for fun. It was a one-time thing. And I'd like to keep it under wraps if you don't mind. If the guys are warming up to me, I don't want it to be for the wrong reason." Not to mention, it probably wouldn't be good for her bosses to know the team psychologist got her groove on with the dance team. "As charming as you are, it'd be nice if you weren't my only patient."

"You think I'm charming?" His eyebrows perked up, but his big smile was interrupted by her warning look. "Okay. I get it. I get it. But you still didn't answer my question."

And she wasn't sure if she should. Information seemed dangerous in his hands. Still, it couldn't hurt to foster a little more rapport. Then maybe Shane "The Wall" Reese would lower a drawbridge and let her in. "That friend I saw this morning, she manages the Summerlin Complex in the Sports Park. She said I could have half the indoor field to myself tonight."

"Oh really? Been meaning to check that place out."

"From what I saw this morning, it's enormous and pretty impressive. I haven't been on a field in too long. I miss drilling, as ridiculous as that sounds."

"Hey, no judgment here. You're talking to a guy who misses busting his ass around the rink in twenty pounds of gear. So far I've been cleared for off-ice training, but all Bill has me doing are stretches and strength tests."

Holy crap, he was actually offering information. About himself. And not under duress. Allie got a grip on the tentative hope rising in her chest and aimed for nonchalant. "Those things are important."

"Yeah, but I've been doing them for weeks. I'm stretched. I'm strong. But I feel like my moves are getting rusty."

Hard to imagine the man across from her with rusty moves. His moves seemed just fine. Too good, in fact. "Have you said that to Bill?"

Reese scoffed. "I tried, but he always says I'll be ready when I'm ready. As if he'll know and I won't."

Her trainer had told her something similar. She remembered those days and how much she hated them. But she wasn't in charge of healing his body. "If you're stronger, he'll see it and get you back in action. That's his job."

"And in the meantime I can't do mine?"

"In the meantime, your job is to do what he says. And what I say." She grinned and almost immediately regretted it. He got that flirty look again, and it was her fault.

"A woman who likes to be in charge. You might be surprised to know I'm okay with that."

A quick image of the lanky goalie tied to her bed flashed through her brain, and she blinked it away. "I ..." Her gaze darted to the clock. "Hey, look—time's up. Aren't you usually racing out of here?"

"I want to go with you."

For a second, the phrasing threw her. It called back middle school days when "going with" someone meant going steady. And the corresponding pre-adolescent thrill rolled through her even though she knew that couldn't be what he intended. "Go with me ..."

"Tonight. To the soccer complex."

Ohhh, no, no, no no. "I don't think so. I'm supposed to make sure you're ready to return to play, not break you worse."

"Okay, for the record, you couldn't break me, Kally. And if you're worried about being liable, I take full responsibility."

"Y'know, even if I had that in writing and notarized, somehow I still think I'd get fired."

"I swear—first hint of pain and I sit on the sidelines. You can even tell me what drills you think would be safe. I just need to be somewhere that isn't here or my house."

She couldn't help a smile. "Sister pushing you to the edge?"

"I passed the edge days ago. This is just as much for her survival as it is mine."

"I don't—"

"I'd hate for the guys to find out about you strip teasing with the dancers."

Her jaw fell open, and panic mixed with *how dare he*, even though the spark in his eyes hinted that he was playing. "It was not a strip tease. And I can't believe you're blackmailing me."

"I'm a desperate man. What if I promise to open up? If you let me go, I'll answer anything you ask."

"I notice you didn't add 'truthfully' in there. And I don't negotiate with terrorists."

"C'mon, please?" His voice lost the joking edge, dropped and softened, but it was his eyes that did her in. She caught a glimpse behind his carefully constructed wall, and it was enough to silence her reservations.

"Fine. You can meet me there at seven, but if I bench you, no debating. And I'm holding you to your promise. Tonight, you're an open book. No diversions."

That trademark charm came back with the dimples in full effect. "I'm all yours."

God help me.

Chapter Six

Tuesday Night

Reese hustled into the house, hoping to miss Saralynn. He'd grabbed some fast food after PT with Bill and wasted as much time as he could so he wouldn't cross paths with his sister for more than a few minutes before meeting up with Allie. Unfortunately, Saralynn was unavoidable. She nearly charged him the minute he was through the door.

"I got it! I got it!"

"The meaning of life? The new issue of *People*?"

"The *internship*! Isn't that great?"

Awesome. Now there'd be no escape. "Yeah. Great. Congrats." He pecked her cheek and squeezed her arm as he maneuvered past, headed for his room.

"Hey, where you going? I thought we could celebrate with a fancy dinner."

"Oh, sorry, Sare. I'm just here to change then heading back out." *Please, let that be enough detail for her.* It wasn't. She trailed him up the stairs and leaned against his bedroom doorframe while he threw on a new t-shirt and cologne.

"You don't usually tart yourself up to go out with the guys. Are you meeting a *girl*?" Way too much interest in her voice. But at least she had moved past guilting him to go celebrate.

"She's not a girl. Well, okay, technically, yeah. But I mean, it's not a date. She's my shrink."

"You're going out after hours with your shrink? Is that allowed? I bet she's pretty."

He faced his sister and sighed. Saralynn had caught the scent, and "Let it go" was not in her vocabulary. He wanted to deny that

Allie was pretty, but the words just wouldn't come out. "Look, it's professional, okay? She played soccer back in the day and has a friend at the Summerlin Complex who gave her half a field for the night. I'm going to cross-train. End of story."

"Uh huh." Saralynn smiled in a way that said she didn't believe a single word. Whatever. If his sister thought he had a date, maybe she'd get off his back about everything else. "Can I meet her?"

"We'll see." His standard answer as far back as he could remember. Telling Saralynn "no" never worked. *We'll see* avoided an argument and her knee-jerk response to authority. He shoved a few clean towels in his duffle and re-filled his water bottle in the master bathroom. "I won't be back too late, okay? Be careful if you go out." He dropped a kiss on top of her head in passing and took the stairs as quickly as he could without risking his ankle.

Going on four years in Vegas, but he'd never made it to the Sports Park even though he passed it occasionally. The lot around Summerlin had several cars, but they were closer to the outdoor fields. He found a spot near the front next to a red Camry. Allie's? Sleek, sporty, dependable. A good fit.

He walked into an empty, cavernous lobby. Where now? A small redhead popped up behind the front desk holding a box of soccer balls and jogged toward a door that led to the fields out back. He cleared his throat, and she swung around to face him, eyes wide.

"Uh, hi. I'm looking for Doctor ... Allie. Allie Kallen?"

"Kally?"

He blinked at her use of the nickname. Then it made sense. He'd bet this was the college friend and teammate. "Yeah, Kally."

The redhead flashed him a mischievous smirk and nodded to his left. "Indoor field."

"Thanks." *Odd.* He frowned and shrugged.

The indoor field was enormous. The ceiling was so high it was easy to forget you *weren't* outside. A springy track circled the

Astroturf, and aluminum benches stretched all the way around. The whole place was empty except for Allie at the far end. She cradled a stack of bright orange pylons and walked hunched over as she set up some kind of obstacle in front of the goal.

As he got closer, he took in her purple nylon shorts and an orange tank top that hung in a Y down her back. Beneath it, a visible purple sports bra. Her soccer cleats weren't new but looked in decent shape. Had she worn them since her injury? Overall, the look wasn't seductive, but damn if it didn't affect him anyway. She may not have played in years, but it was hard to imagine her in any better shape. Her ponytail swung between her shoulder blades as she walked toward her gym bag. When she bent to get her water bottle, he couldn't look away.

Unfortunately, his gaze was still angled there when she faced him. She coughed on some water and wiped her mouth with the back of her wrist. "Jeez. You need a bell around your neck or something. How long have you been standing there?"

"Not long. Sorry. Didn't mean to scare you."

"Uh huh." Her smile diffused the tension, and she nodded behind her to the bench with her duffle. "Why don't you put your stuff down, and we'll warm up?"

If she only knew how warm he already was. But that's not what she meant. He cleared his throat, nodded, and followed orders while trying to get his libido under control. Clearly, it had been too long for him, but after the injury, women had been the last thing on his mind. Until now.

Allie stood to the side of the pylons and stretched her arms over her head. Reese mirrored her stance, trying not to stare at the narrow band of skin exposed by her rising tank top. When she bent over to touch her toes, he had to close his eyes to remain a gentleman. The next set of stretches were on the ground, the ones he'd been most familiar with in PT. He could do them in his sleep—probably did—so he went through the motions without thinking too much and watched her instead. She was graceful. More like a ballerina than a soccer player. He really didn't know much about her. That needed to change.

"So, where'd you grow up?"

She looked at him with playful suspicion and resumed stretching. "Near Pittsburgh. Won a soccer scholarship to Stanford. After I graduated and couldn't play anymore, I got an assistantship at Alaska Pacific University for my master's in counseling. And then Boston U for my Ph.D."

"Impressive resume."

"And yet, I was woefully unprepared for you."

"Hey." He narrowed his eyes.

She laughed, and any remnant of insult disappeared. "Kidding. Mostly. All right, get up, and we'll start drilling. I want you to go slow. I mean it. And you promised to listen, remember?" She rose first and offered him a hand.

"Yeah, yeah." He considered getting up without her help. He didn't need it. But he couldn't resist the contact even for a few seconds. Her skin was warm and soft, but her grip was strong. It was hard finding the motivation to let go.

• • •

Allie never thought he'd accept her help up, so when he did, it paralyzed her for a few seconds. His hand was a little rough and felt like it could crush hers even though she was no weakling. Except, he wasn't crushing. He wasn't letting go, either. He pulled her forward a step, and her heartbeat sped up. His cologne filled her head. Fierce by A&F. Fitting. Intoxicating. The intent in his eyes turned her mouth dry. The dynamics were different here. In her office, they had clearly defined roles. Doctor. Patient. Outside of that neutral zone …

"Hey." She broke the tension with a smile she hoped didn't convey her nerves. "I said no diversions."

The slight curve of his mouth nearly did her in, but apparently he decided to take pity and let his hand fall back to his side. "You're right. Show me the first drill."

Drills. Right. The reason they were there. The *only* reason. She felt guilty for even the little bit of unethical flirting. Burying and repressing things went against the grain in her line of work, but in this case, those were her best options. She nodded and stood at the end of the row of pylons. "Okay, you'll serpentine around the cones down and back. I'm going to go a little fast, but I want you walking. If I see so much as a hop in your step, you'll be guarding our stuff on the bench for the rest of the night. Got it?"

"Yes, Coach."

She chose to ignore his amusement and the way his biceps bulged when he folded his arms over his chest. Instead, she focused on her feet as she darted in and out of the cones. It had been so long, but muscle memory took over, and after the first few, she was flying. She even kept her concentration when Reese whistled, clapped, and yelled, "Go Kally!" Down the row and back in under a minute. She bent, hands on knees, and caught her breath.

"That's pretty impressive. You know it's gonna kill me to be outpaced by a girl."

She stepped aside so he could take her place. "My top concern is keeping you in one piece. Kicking your butt is a side benefit."

He gave a small, mirthless laugh then started down the row. Three cones in, he said, "This is humiliating."

"This is our deal. Eyes on your feet."

Reese shook his head with mock resignation but did as he was told. It was easier to study him when he wasn't staring back at her. He wore green, nylon gym shorts to his knees and a black Sinners locker room t-shirt—the kind just for the team and not sold in the arena. Running shoes—not cleats, but he wouldn't be moving fast enough to need the extra traction anyway.

He did look funny walking in and out of the cones, but she didn't need to point that out. Aside from the turtle's pace, his balance looked better. He put equal weight on both feet without hesitation. Bill would clear him soon, and then it'd just depend on her decision. But something seemed off. Maybe it was his reaction—or lack thereof—when she asked why he got injured. He'd simply shut down, and that always flagged a deeper issue. Time for him to live up to the other part of their deal.

"So, Mr. Open Book, I believe you owe me some honest answers."

He turned around at the last cone and started back, glancing at her briefly. "Oh … right. Ask away."

No excitement, but no refusal either. Workable. "You've been playing with Phlynn your whole life. How'd things change when he retired and moved to management?"

He hesitated, then resumed weaving in and out of the pylons, keeping his gaze on his feet. "I miss him, if that's what you're asking. Guy's been a brother to me my whole life on and off the ice. Things didn't change much at first. We still hung out. He'd come down and bust my balls at practice from the bench when Coach would let him."

Easy to see where this was going, and it broke her heart a little. "And then?"

"And then …" He finished walking through the cones and faced her. "He became GM. Had to start making hard calls. The team hit a mid-season slump, and I saw him less. We made it to the playoffs but barely. Then all the trade rumors."

The pain in his eyes was almost enough to make her look away. To touch him now, even a comforting hand on the elbow, would make him feel weak and close him down. Instead, she let a silent moment pass before she nodded toward the goal. "I'm going in.

I need you to stand at the penalty mark," she pointed to a spot designated with a neon soccer ball, "and try to get past me."

His eyebrows went up. "That's it? You're not going to poke and prod and pick me apart?"

"I'm not trying to pick you apart. I'm trying to put you back together." She winked, then took her place in goal.

He stared after her as if he were waiting for her to change her mind. When she didn't, he shrugged and stood a few feet behind the ball.

"Don't get too much of a wind-up. Walk to it and kick with your good foot. Don't put too much strain on your bad ankle."

"You come off all concerned, but you just want me to go easy on you."

That pricked at her competitive streak, but so far the teasing was good-natured. If she accepted his half-hearted challenge, the game would be on, and if they both went all-out, they'd end up sharing a room at Mountain View Hospital. "You gonna kick or what?"

He laughed, approached the ball comically slow then kicked high and to her right. Because he hadn't put his full power behind it, she was able to knock it away with a skip and a jump. She kicked it back to him, and they continued that way with the occasional joke or friendly jibe.

When it was his turn in net, she ordered him to stand with his feet shoulder-width apart and not move anything except his arms. Although she couldn't say it went over well, he still accepted it better than she'd expected. When they stopped for water, she checked her watch. Almost ten. "Guess we should call it a night." She wiped the sweat from her face with a towel and watched as he did the same.

"Yeah. Guess so." No motivation in his tone, and he made no move for his duffle. Sweat molded his shirt to his wide, muscled chest. He stared at her with the same intensity from earlier, and it affected every inch of her body. So dangerous. So easy to cross a line. The scary thing? For the first time in her life, she actually wanted to.

He leaned toward her.

Temptation momentarily glued her to the spot, but self-preservation allowed her to take a step back and scoop up her things. "So I'll see you Thursday?"

Reese glanced at the ground and slid a hand over the back of his neck. "Yeah, see you Thursday."

A few steps away, and she could breathe again.

"Kally?"

She looked over her shoulder, knowing she shouldn't.

"Thank you."

Two words, but they conveyed a lot, and she understood on every level. He'd let his guard down, so she returned the favor and smiled without reservation. "You're welcome." She didn't have to look again to know he watched her all the way out. Doctor Kallen tsk tsked. Allie enjoyed the moment.

Chapter Seven

Culinary Dropout looked like a lot of Vegas restaurants, conveniently located adjacent to the hotel's casino and pool, but it did have more of a pub feel. Upscale but still comfortable and kind of funky. British flags and antlers adorned the walls, and ornate, crystal chandeliers glittered from the ceiling. Allie sat across from Mac; the better to watch the sunburned tourists in over-sized t-shirts and socks with sandals.

"Kind of feels like you're on permanent vacation, doesn't it?" Mac grinned then looked back at her menu.

"Actually, yeah. It's kind of weird, but I think I like it. Still feel like a tourist myself."

"Me, too, in places like this, and I've lived here for ten years now. But world-class food is worth a little cheese. Speaking of, they have a cheese tray here that's to die for. But I think I'm feeling … ooo! Grilled artichokes!"

Allie laughed. Mac looked radiantly happy. It was a nice change from long faces and sob stories. Not that she didn't love her job, but constantly being around pain and sadness took its toll.

A waiter stopped by, but the only indicator was the apron around his waist. He had a shaved head save for a neon orange Mohawk styled into five stiff spikes. He wore a faded band t-shirt, expensive-looking jeans with holes, and black CAT boots. "Evenin' ladies. M'name's Slade, and I'll be taking care of you tonight. What can I get you to drink?"

Mac glanced up, totally unfazed. "Just water for me. But Kally, you *have* to try the clown punch."

Allie squinted at her friend and pursed her lips. The pieces clicked in place, but she held her tongue. "What is clown punch?"

Slade cleared his throat. "It's flor de cana, peach brandy, St. Germain, and orange juice. Fruity but packs a punch like the name. Quite tasty."

It did sound good. After her morning, maybe a little punch was just what she needed. "I'll try it, but can I also have a tall glass of water?"

Slade, who appeared maybe six foot three, looked about to say *I'm right here* but must have read the *No thank you* on her face. "You got it. Can I put any appetizers in?"

"Grilled artichokes!" Mac smiled shyly. "Please."

"You got it." Slade beamed at her then headed for the bar.

Allie grinned. "So when are you due?"

Mac's eyes went wide, and her mouth fell open a little. "Shoulda known you'd figure it out before I could say. November. We're waiting until the second trimester to announce it."

"*You* ordering water was kind of a tip-off. Congratulations, girl!"

"Thanks. I guess I could hold my own back in college, huh? But you know what? I don't even miss it."

"Good for you. I'm happy for you."

"I'm over the moon, Kally. Never really saw myself as a mom, but the title's growing on me along with the stomach."

"Ohh, you're not showing, and you know it."

Slade reappeared with a tray and handed out the waters before setting the clown punch in front of Allie. A big goblet with what looked like straight orange juice on the bottom and two inches of froth on top. "Pomegranate foam," Slade supplied. "I suggest eating it with a spoon, then sipping the drink."

That turned out to be good advice. *Slowly* sipping, because wow, did it pack a wallop. Mac ordered a burger with her name on it—literally—the M.A.C. burger. Allie ordered the fried chicken with honey biscuit, mashed potatoes, and gravy. They reminisced about college and caught up on the lost years. And when Mac clearly couldn't hold back any more, they got to Reese.

"All right. Dish. That was Shane Reese looking for you last night, wasn't it?"

"You know him?"

"Kally, I've been following the Sinners since their inception three years ago. Not many professional sports in Vegas, and hockey is pretty much soccer on ice with sticks. He's cute."

Allie rolled her eyes. "He's a pain in the ass."

"Ha! He's a *cute* pain in the ass. Your mouth twitched. Total tell."

Did it? Okay, Reese *might* be cute, but it didn't matter. "That's irrelevant. He's my patient."

"That's a damn shame. The man is built like Adonis. And that smile. And those eyes!"

"Hey, you're taken, remember?" Allie laughed and took a big sip of clown punch. The world tilted a little.

"I'm just saying. For you, I mean. What are the others like?"

"I wouldn't know."

"But ..."

"Yeah, team sports psychologist. You'd think I'd treat the whole team, right? But they're terrified of me, at least professionally. They think I can read minds or something. I had a brief interaction with Dylan Cole when he walked me to my car one night. He seemed nice."

Mac gaped. "They seriously don't talk to you? Except Reese? What do you do the rest of the time?"

"Counsel the cheerleaders. Sorry, dance team. They're nice girls but have a lot of issues. That's what I did today. Back-to-back sessions. I'm not sure I'm supposed to, but I might as well do *something* to earn the paycheck until the rest of the team opens up. Or is ordered to see me. My role is to be at their disposal.

Problem is they think I'm disposable." The dancers, however, were desperate to share their stories. That morning, Bianca cried for an hour as she relayed the details of her absent father. It was a sad, running theme throughout the day—and heartbreaking. Amazing how much sense of self was tied into that delicate father-daughter relationship.

"Kally?" Mac waved a hand in front of her face.

Allie blinked the fog away and shook her head, but the clown punch had her feeling warm and fuzzy. "Sorry. Got distracted."

"Think it's time to call it a night." Mac slung her purse over her shoulder. "Why don't I take you home, and tomorrow morning I'll give you a ride to your car at the complex? Pick you up at eight?"

"Yeah, sounds good, thanks. Wow. Clown punch."

Mac laughed, a familiar tinkle of mirth and mischief. "Sorry, should have warned you better. You were gulping it toward the end. It's sweet, so you don't notice the haze until it hits you full force."

"Mmhmm."

The ride home was a blur, but Allie felt a little more clear-headed as she set the coffee timer, took some pre-emptive Aleve, then dropped into bed. She had a cute goalie to face tomorrow and a mission to accomplish before that.

Chapter Eight

A good, hard sleep cleared the haze, and Allie felt fresh when Mac dropped her off at her car. That was lucky, because today would take focus, clarity, and patience. Instead of hitting up her office first thing, she headed for the team's video room where they kept game footage. There had to be something more to Reese's injury, and if he didn't want to fess up, at least the camera wouldn't lie.

At this hour, the team was still practicing, and Reese wouldn't be in until later. Even so, she peeked up and down the hallway before knocking on the video coordinator's door.

"Come in," came a muted but distracted-sounding reply from inside.

Allie pushed on the door, and it swung open. A middle-age man in a Sinners tracksuit sat hunched in front of a wall of screens, adjusting dials and knobs. "Hi. You're Justin Miller, right? I'm—"

"Dr. Alexandra Kallen, or Kally as they say. I've heard of you." He spun on his swivel chair and extended his hand with a wry smile.

She winced but accepted the shake. "They talk about me?"

"Oh, don't worry," he said, spinning back to face the screens. "It's not personal. They're just afraid of someone poking around in their brains. They like to consider themselves impenetrable."

"I could go Freud with that, but I won't."

Justin snorted and patted the stool beside him. "You're all right by me, kid. Have a seat. What can I do for you?"

Allie perched on the edge of the stool, messenger bag in her lap. "I'd like to see footage from the night Reese got hurt."

He nodded. "Figured you would at some point. He not being exactly forthcoming?"

"Not exactly. I just want to see for myself." Reese wasn't lying or even purposefully withholding. Okay, maybe some of that, but he definitely wasn't admitting to himself what happened.

"Gotcha. Tell you what. I've never seen a player take an injury this bad before. High ankle sprains are frustrating 'cause symptoms fluctuate like with concussions, but Reese has been a black cloud." Justin clicked around on the main monitor, a computer screen, and pulled up the game, then slid a cursor along the bottom, scanning ahead to the right moment. "Here we go."

It played out so fast. Reese stood in goal, angled against the right post with his glove up as play went into the corner. A Kings forward shot a quick pass to the left, and the receiving player fired off a one-timer. Reese had time to slide into position, but he looked at Chekov, the three hundred pound Russian, who dove to screen Reese and ended up on top of him. They went down, and the puck hit the back of the net.

"It didn't count. They called goaltender interference and took the point back, but the Sinners lost that game anyway." Justin shook his head.

"Can you run it again? Slower?"

He nodded and played it back tick-by-tick.

In slow motion, Reese's hesitation was clearer. Damn. "Can I see the goal cam?"

"Sure." Some more clicks, a little scanning, and the moment played again, this time from behind Reese. From this angle, he didn't just hesitate. He *stopped*. It was almost as if he were looking for a way out of having to make the save.

"Thanks, Justin. Can you burn this on a DVD for me?"

"You got it."

• • •

For the first time, Reese actually looked forward to his session with Allie. The other night was on loop in his brain. He'd dropped his guard. Hell, he'd forgotten to put it up. Just playing around with her, laughing and BSing, he'd almost forgotten about his injury entirely. He'd sure forgotten to be angry about it. And it hadn't felt like cross training. In fact, it was more like a date. The best date of his life. *Shit*. He was in trouble.

He knocked on her office door then stepped inside. She had her back to him as she poked at a TV on a rolling stand—the kind Nealy used in the locker room to show them game footage. "We watching a movie today, Teach?"

She glanced at him over her shoulder, and one side of her mouth quirked up. Not the full, untempered smile he was used to. Uh oh.

"You're not gonna like this. But I want to see what you think."

His throat clicked when he tried to swallow. He sat on the sofa and leaned his forearms on his knees. It could only be one thing. He hadn't watched the tape. Nealy'd tried to persuade him, but he didn't want to. What was the point? He'd lived it. He knew what happened. "Is this really necessary? It's over. I'm healing. Not hitting anything or anyone. Practically cured."

Her half-smile turned into a smirk, and she sat next to him on the couch. There wasn't a lot of room—he took up most of it—so her thigh pressed lightly against his, and their shoulders touched. Her Creamsicle perfume would have calmed him under other circumstances, but his heart was trying to set a speed record.

She pushed play on the remote. Almost a month ago, but every second felt fresh. He watched the Kings set up the shot that would take him down. It was over in a blink, but he breathed hard as if the memory had taken physical exertion. Pain jolted in his ankle as he saw himself fall, but it was a phantom pain. A tremor ran through his fingers, and he curled them into loose fists. "Well." He cleared his throat. "That was fun."

"I know this is hard, but I need you to see it."

The screen shot changed to the goalie cam, and the moment replayed, but this time in slow motion. He saw the pass then watched himself focus on Chekov instead of the King with the puck. The image hit him like a truck. That couldn't possibly be him standing there. He'd dived to make the save as soon as he saw the shot coming. Hadn't he? Allie hit pause. He expected questions, maybe a lecture, but she was quiet.

"You want to know why I looked away."

She didn't answer, just stared at him patiently, her expression neutral.

He sighed and shoved a hand back through his hair. "I'm having a fucking *Body Snatchers* moment right now. I don't remember doing that." He glanced at her. "Sorry."

The corner of her mouth twitched like she might want to smile, so his language didn't bother her. "You really don't remember it happening like that?"

"No. I—" He stopped as it started to make sense. "You knew. You knew I was … what, repressing something? That's why you wanted me to watch the tape."

"I had a feeling."

He stood up, his pulse pounding harder. "Why does it matter how it happened? It happened. It's over. I didn't need to see this. I don't need to re-live it. I don't need to examine it. I don't know why you thought this would change anything."

Before she could reply, he left. He didn't slam the door, but he didn't close it gently either. His temples pounded, and phantom or not, his ankle ached. Anger burned through him, but he had nowhere to direct it. Instead of hitting another wall, he headed for the workout room and the heavy bag.

Chapter Nine

Allie sat behind her desk, her stare unfocused. Yesterday's session was a disaster, but that hadn't been a complete shocker. The intensity of his reaction was a little surprising. Hurt, anger, frustration; all emotions she hated to see on Reese's face, and she'd put them there. But she had to. He couldn't get past his mistake if he refused to admit he'd made it. She wouldn't repeat her own mistake with her last patient from her internship with the Providence Bruins.

Caleb Johansson, only twenty-two when he got his second serious concussion, had to see her three days a week for a month. On top of being checked out by a team of medical doctors, the Bruins had enlisted her help to make sure he was game ready. He was symptom-free, or so he'd convinced her, and ready to handle the stress of returning to play.

She could see him clearly, sitting across from her, schooling his face into a lop-sided smile, willing confidence into his eyes. Why hadn't she looked past it? Seen the anxiety inside and known he wasn't ready? It hadn't been just her okay that sent him back to the ice. No one blamed her when he had his head down in the corner and took a check that came with a career-ending concussion. Hard to escape her own guilt though.

A quiet knock, so quiet she wasn't sure she hadn't imagined it, brought her back to the present. A second later, Dylan Cole slid inside and eased the door closed behind him. He looked around like he expected to get caught, his posture tense and fidgety. When he focused on her, his shaky smile offered an apology.

"Uh, hi. Sorry to drop in. If you're busy, I can—I should just—"

"Cole." She nodded to the couch. "Sit." *Holy cow.* A player sought her out. Of his own volition. She sat still as a statue so he wouldn't spook.

The rookie perched on the very edge of the cushion closest to the door, forearms on his knees, looking around her office as if he were memorizing every detail. Sometimes it was best to keep quiet and let the patient talk first. She gave him a few minutes of silence, but his urge to bolt broadcasted across his young face.

"How've you been?" An easy enough opener and not too probing.

He seemed to realize how comical his posture was, and he sat back slowly. When the couch didn't bite, the line of his shoulders relaxed a fraction, and he shot her another apologetic smile. "Guess I'm a little jumpy. The guys don't know I'm here. I wanted to … get your opinion."

And now the nerves made sense. Hang with the outcast, and you might get evil cooties. But he'd come anyway. She fought to keep her smile small and leaned back in her chair, keeping her posture and tone as laidback as possible, forgoing the usual pen and paper. "You got it."

He relaxed a bit more. "This is my first season as captain."

The youngest captain in NHL history. Instead of pointing that out, she simply nodded. Easy to see where this was going.

"Guys have been really good about it mostly. I mean, we have a couple graybeards, and they have a lot more experience. My numbers are good, I had a lucky season last year, but … I don't know."

"You have a season's worth of experience under your belt now. Do you still feel unprepared to lead your team?"

"It's not that. I don't doubt myself exactly, I just don't know if I deserve it yet." He said the last staring at the pumpkin seeds on the coffee table. A hotshot on the ice and more humble than any kid she'd ever met.

"You're the top scorer for the Sinners and in line for the Art Ross Trophy for scoring in the league. You have even more assists than goals, so you know how to put your team first. From what I've seen, you don't let your ego get in the way, and you get along with everyone."

"You know my stats. You a fan, Doc?" No flirtation, just apparent relief to change the topic even for a second.

She smiled at the stall and lifted a shoulder. "Gotta know my team."

That got a genuine smile from him, and he looked even younger.

"You said mostly the guys have been good about it. Anyone who hasn't?"

He ducked his head and shrugged.

"Not a word leaves this room. Doctor-patient confidentiality."

He hesitated, still seemingly reluctant to rat out his brothers but met her gaze as if steeling himself. "I think Reese has a problem with me. I don't know what. I don't think I did anything. Yeah, he's had a problem with everyone lately, but maybe me especially? I don't get it because we got along good last year."

Things crystallized a little more, not just about Cole but about Reese, too. How much to say? She wanted to reassure the kid, but she could only share so much about Reese without breaking code. "I can tell you this: it's not about you. I guarantee it. Give him some space, and he'll come around."

"You think so?" The tentative hope in his puppy dog eyes was heartbreaking. It really killed him that a member of his team didn't like him.

At the moment, Reese appeared far from revelation, but he *would* come around if he didn't want to get traded. "I do. Just give him a little time. And Cole?"

He lifted his head, his expression earnest and open.

"You're a good captain. They wouldn't have chosen you otherwise. You've earned it. And you earn it more every game."

That unguarded smile returned, and he pushed to his feet. "Thanks, Kally."

"My door's always open."

He waved and peered into the hallway before slipping out, his exit as stealthy as his entrance. Putting aside the offense of being slated the girl no one wanted to be seen with, it was a productive Friday. Now if only Reese could get out of his own way.

Chapter Ten

Sunday, April 28th

"That's a bad face." Saralynn made this helpful observation seated atop the island in the kitchen, kicking her high heels against the side and peeling a banana. She wore black pants that were a little too close-fitting to be professional and a white dress shirt with a green pinstripe that needed one more button closed at the top. Her *intern outfit*.

Reese dropped his duffle in the hall and opened the fridge. "I'm not in the mood, Sare."

"You're in *a* mood, Mopey. You have been for days. Since Thursday, actually. What's up?"

Explaining everything to his baby sister marked the bottom of his to-do list, but she had that look. If he locked himself in his room as he'd done the last few days, she wouldn't ignore him anymore. He'd bet she'd stand outside and knock until he opened. It was a miracle she'd waited this long to put her foot down. "My shrink made me watch the footage of my injury." Put that simply, it sounded like he was being a gigantic baby. Whatever.

Saralynn arched a brow. "And?"

"Look, I didn't need to see it, okay? I was there the first time. What good did it do to make me watch the most painful moment in my career?"

"Maybe you just don't like what you saw."

He closed the fridge hard and opened his mouth. Nothing came out. If he denied what she said, it'd be a straight-out lie. He *didn't* like what he saw. Didn't want to believe it. Didn't want to think about it. Not that that stopped him. He leaned his hands on the island counter and stared down at the white-gray marble, shaking his head. "I just don't understand. I don't understand what I did or why I did it. I just *stood* there, looking the wrong way when I should have been making a save."

"Why were you looking the wrong way?"

"I don't *know.*"

"Hey, just the sister." She held her hands up palms out, and he softened.

"Sorry."

"If this is you with kid gloves, I can only imagine what you said to the shrink."

Allie. He rubbed his face. She didn't deserve the outburst. Maybe he did need to see the video. She was just doing her job. "Fuck."

"Language."

"Sorry."

Saralynn laughed. "I was kidding. But really, you need to apologize to her."

"How do I do that? I was an embarrassing ass."

His sister tilted her head. "Make it personal. Do you know anything about her?"

"Not really."

"Do you know someone who does?"

· · ·

Monday, April 29th

Big gesture. It would take a big gesture to make up for the way he acted last week. This was the only way. Humiliating as it might be, the one person in Vegas who knew more than the Cliffs Notes of Allie Kallen was her college teammate, and Reese was about to beg her mercy.

At noon, the soccer complex sat empty, as he'd hoped. And to his relief, a short redhead stood behind the front desk. Her nametag read Dana.

He pushed his hands in his pockets and braced himself. "Hi. I talked to you the other day. My name's—"

"Shane Reese, goalie for the Sinners."

"Y-yeah." Did she just know that, or had she and Allie talked about him? In a personal way, it flattered him. If they talked about how his career was in the tank … but Dana wasn't looking at him with judgment. Amusement, maybe. "I was hoping I could get your help."

"*Me?*" Her tiny eyebrows went up, and she grinned. Fan. Okay, so maybe they hadn't talked about him.

"You'd be the only one who could help. I wasn't the best patient last week. I lost my cool, and it wasn't Allie's fault. I want to apologize, maybe get her favorite candy or something, but I don't know what it is. Thought you would." Plus, payback for Allie finding out about his love of pumpkin seeds sounded pretty tempting.

"You yelled at Kally?"

"I feel awful—"

"No, you yelled at Kally and your shins are still intact." She leaned on the desk to look at his legs. "Girl can kick."

He bit the inside of his cheek, fighting a laugh. "Yeah, I deserved it, too. I want to make it up to her."

"You should. She's a good person. All right. Let's see." Dana pursed her lips and glanced off to the side. "Back in college she was hooked on chocolate-covered gummy bears. Always had a few before games and at halftime."

"That's perfect. Thanks, Dana."

Confusion wrinkled her brows before she looked down at her nametag. "Oh, right. Sorry, should have introduced myself.

Dana Sickavish, but I go by Mac because my last name used to be MacGuire. Even my husband calls me Mac."

"My family calls me Reese." They shared a grin, and he felt a little more at ease. "I really appreciate this."

"No problem. But maybe work on your cool so future apologies aren't necessary."

"Goal of my life at the moment."

Chapter Eleven

Tuesday, April 30th

"Let go of the problems that don't belong to you. You don't need that stress. It's okay to say no sometimes." Allie walked around her desk and handed Shelly a much needed tissue to wipe away the hundreds of dollars of makeup streaming down the dancer's face.

"You're right," Shelly hiccupped. "I know you're right. It's just hard. I don't want to let anyone down."

"You're no good to anyone if you don't take care of yourself first."

Shelly nodded and was mid sniffle as the door opened. She started, hands flying to her face when the interrupter turned out to be male.

Allie would have bet ten to one odds he wouldn't show today. He had one arm behind his back, and he stopped cold when he saw the crying woman on the couch. His eyes darted to the clock on the wall. He looked like a statue, focused on Allie.

"Oh, sorry. I—ah …"

"No, it's okay. We're just wrapping up. Shelly, we'll talk later?"

"Yeah. Thanks." The dancer ducked out with her head down.

Reese closed the door and just stood there for a minute, clearly confused about what he'd walked in on.

"I counsel the dance team. It's informal; they drop in when they need to. I know it may not be covered in my job description, but—"

"No, I think it's good. People need to talk, and you want to listen." His expression softened, and was that a tinge of admiration in his eyes? At least it wasn't anger. "I'm really sorry about Thursday."

Stupid, but a giant weight lifted from her chest. Why did this feel more like making up with a boyfriend than making peace with a patient? "It's okay."

"No, it's not. I took everything out on you, and you were just helping me see something I'd blocked."

"You're a goalie. Blocking things is reflexive. Really, it's okay. I'm used to it. You know what they say about messengers? Therapists learn to wear a bulletproof vest." His words still meant more than they should, and her inner ethics police issued a warning.

"Call me Shane." It came out in a quick blurt, and even he seemed momentarily surprised by it, but then his eyes turned pleading.

No one called him Shane. It meant *that* much that she forgave him? The girl in her was touched by the gesture. The doctor saw how it could blur boundaries. But how could she say no? He was offering an olive branch. Snapping it in half would halt their progress. His progress. "Okay."

The tension slid from him, drooping his shoulders. "I, uh, came prepared just in case." He brought around the arm that had been behind his back, revealing a white tin pail with the Sugar Factory logo on the front.

"What did you …" She accepted the gift and peered inside. The iconic yellow rubber ducky sat atop a decorative bag of chocolate covered gummy bears. Her lips parted, and she blinked twice. "How did you know?"

A somewhat guilty smile turned up one corner of his mouth. "I asked Mac. I hope that's not too stalker. It's just, she knows you, and I wanted to get something personal."

It *was* above and beyond what a patient would do, and it felt like more than an apology. Encouraging him could be dangerous, but refusing the gift could shut him down again. A thin moral line; where both answers were right and wrong. She kept her smile small and polite and set the pail in the center of her desk. "Thank you."

Disappointment tinged his eyes briefly at the muted reaction, but he took a seat in the middle of the couch. "I was an ass."

"Happens to the best of us. You should have seen me when *my* shrink played the video."

"*You?* You probably took a sip of tea and said, 'Thank you for the enlightenment. I totally understand.'"

Allie laughed louder than she meant to, and she leaned over, holding onto an edge of her wingback chair. After a good minute of trying to stop, she took a seat and wiped under her eyes. "I seriously wish I had *that* on tape. It would make you feel better. No, this calm, level-headed masterpiece before you took years of work and classes. Let's just say my exit was less graceful than yours."

"No way." His smile was a little shy, but the embarrassment peeled back bit by bit, and he seemed back to the usual banter. Good.

"Oh yeah. Not my best moment. But you know what? Once I got past being offended, I realized it was a good thing. If I could take responsibility for my injury and own my mistake, I knew I could avoid making it again. In my case, I ended up retiring, but it's different for you. We need to figure out why you looked at Chekov." She edged around and lowered into the chair but leaned back and kept her posture loose.

Shane stared at nothing for a minute then glanced at her and cocked his head. "Wait a minute. Do you already know? If you don't mind, could you just tell me? I know it's shrink policy to try and get the patients to find the answers on their own, but I'm kind of wiped, and I swear I won't storm out again."

She shook her head. "I have a theory. What if I meet you half way?"

He groaned.

"Well, let's look at it. This hasn't been your best season by your own admission. What's different about this year?"

"You mean Phlynn. What does he have to do with it?"

"Think about it. You've played with Phlynn your entire life. You've never been on the ice without him except for minor injuries here and there. When he retired, it messed with your focus, at least on a subconscious level. Maybe you felt jinxed without him."

"Are you saying playing with Phlynn was like a superstition? I lost my lucky rabbit's foot and couldn't play anymore? Come on. I'm a professional athlete."

"*And* a goalie. If anyone knows about superstition, it's us." She lifted the candy pail and let it swing from her fingers.

A smile twitched at the corners of his mouth. "Mac told me you had to eat them before and in the middle of every game. But Phlynn is not a gummy bear."

"No. He's much bigger and actually affected what happened on the ice. He was the captain, the leader, and his exit has affected other players, not just you. The guys didn't play as well in front of you this season, but I know it's easy to hoard all the blame when you're the one guarding the net. And then the trade rumors …"

He looked at her. Blinked. "You think I wanted Chekov to snap my ankle so I wouldn't get traded?"

"On some level. Maybe."

Shane scoffed, but there wasn't much heart behind it. Then he went quiet, and she could see the gears turning. "Holy shit."

She hesitated to give him space. "And word is, you haven't gotten along the best with Cole this season. Do you think he's a bad captain?"

His brows furrowed, and he frowned. "No. Kid's got chops. Knows the game."

"But?"

It took a minute then realization dawned. "He's not …"

"Right. And that's not his fault. He'll never be Phlynn, but he's not trying to. The captaincy was offered to him. He had to take it. Cole's finding his own way."

Shane winced. "I have been hard on him." He scrubbed a hand over his face then peered through his fingers. "They're not paying you enough."

"Tell me about it."

His grin came back, full and brilliant, showing her white teeth and dimples. "All right. So I make peace with the guys. And Phlynn. And I'm ready to go back?"

"That's the theory. If Trainer Bill fills out his portion of the form, I'll sign on the dotted line."

He looked like he might say something then changed his mind. Instead, he pushed to his feet and lingered by the door. "Thanks, Kally. For putting up with me."

Yeah, there was truth in that, but it hadn't been all bad. "My pleasure." If he knew just how much, they'd both be in trouble. "With any luck, you won't need to see me again."

He paused half in, half out the door and shot her one more heart-stopping smile. "In here, anyway."

Chapter Twelve

Friday, May 4th

Shane sat on the bench in the locker room, tying his skates. His fingers threaded the laces on autopilot. It freed his mind for more important things. Like stressing the hell out. His heart had been pounding since Nealy took him aside two days ago and said she was putting him in tonight. His coach might be tiny and, well, female, but she was more terrifying than any man he'd ever met. Not that she could physically hurt him—he didn't think—but she was fierce about the sport, and in some twisted way, the whole team was afraid of disappointing her.

His teammates dressed all around him, joking and laughing, loose and relaxed. They would be after three wins. This series was all but in the bag. They'd welcomed him back, and he'd accepted it with a good dose of crow for how he'd treated them. No signs they were nervous to have him in net, but that didn't help *his* nerves. He hadn't talked to Phlynn, but that shouldn't matter. He understood his issues. Wasn't that enough? It better be. A win tonight would send them to the conference finals. No pressure there. The back-up goalie, Kade Simkins, had barely made a mistake since taking over. Must be nice.

Stop. That kind of thinking wouldn't get him anywhere. According to Allie, if he made peace with the guys, his play would return to normal. *God, please.* The thought of letting his team down, of not being able to get back to his game, had bile rising in his throat. Jacey came in and gave the usual rah-rah, but he didn't hear the individual words. He only knew the speech was over when the door closed behind her.

"You okay, man?" Dylan Cole stood before him, suited up and ready to go. Kid probably didn't even have to shave yet. But he *was* a hell of a player and a strong captain.

"I'm good, thanks."

"Good to have you back, Reesey." Cole clapped him on the shoulder with a big glove and headed to pep talk Kevin Scott and Ben Collier.

Guilt and regret left a bad taste in his mouth yet again for how he'd taken out his frustration on the rookie. Cole wasn't even really a rookie anymore. He was just the baby of the team, so they all still thought of him that way even with his new leadership role.

Nealy pushed into the room, and everyone fell quiet. A nuclear presence in an itty bitty package. She stood by the doors to the tunnel and clasped her hands behind her back. "One more win. That's all we need to make it to the conference finals. Don't get cocky. The Sharks have their back against the wall. They will not fucking roll over for you. They will not go down easy. Don't let up for a damn second. Are you ready?"

Barks of "Yeah!" and "Hell yeah!" echoed around the room. Shane didn't join in. He stared at his blocker glove, hoping to find the secrets of the universe. Nealy opened the doors to the tunnel and watched her team file down to the ice. Cole stood opposite their coach, patting players on the back as they passed. Shane was the last out, and Cole gave him two pats. Nealy gave him a hard-to-define but intimidating stare. He swallowed hard and kept going.

• • •

Allie settled into her seat in the packed arena, sandwiched between a large man in face paint and a couple making out. Not the best vantage point, but she always had a free ticket to games, and this one was important. Shane didn't know she was there, and that was for the best. It would only psych him out more. Still, she had to see how he did his first game back. If it didn't go well, he'd show up at her door, and she wanted to be prepared.

One minute until game time. Something vibrated in her pocket, and she had an irrational second of panicked wiggling before *cell phone* popped into her mind. No one noticed. She held the phone to one ear, and covered the other. "Hello?"

"Dr. Kallen? This is Nealy Windham. Are you in the arena?"

Nealy? She'd met the famous coach briefly before she started but hadn't spoken to her since. The woman's time was precious during playoffs, and it hadn't seemed necessary.

"I'm here. I'm in the crowd."

"I want you closer. Can you meet me by the locker room? Fast as you can." Her serious tone didn't leave room for argument.

"Sure. I'll be right there." Allie ended the call and maneuvered her way to the aisle. She darted up the steps to the main concourse, her heartbeat matching her footsteps. What could Nealy want? Was something wrong with Shane? But he was out on the ice. He looked okay. She upped her pace and used her key card to take the elevator to the basement.

Nealy waited, a small woman with a shockingly large presence. Confidence, determination, and a no-nonsense attitude radiated from her. "Let's go," she said, already heading for the locker room. "I want you to watch Reese up close. I know he wants to be ready. I just want your professional opinion while you watch him play."

Allie followed her through the doors and gagged at the first wave of sweat-sock stench. She covered her nose and mouth and jogged to keep up with Nealy. The mighty sprite, as the guys called her, pushed through the next set of doors and led the way down the carpet runner toward the ice. When they got to the entrance, Nealy touched her shoulder. "Stay here and keep an eye on him." The Sinners' coach winked, then made her way to the player's box to stand behind her team and start giving orders.

A giant, hulking, mountain of a security guard witnessed the exchange and favored Allie with an amused smile. She returned it even with her pulse still pounding. For a second, it was Caleb's first game back all over again, and the old guilt had her leaning on the baseboard supporting the Plexiglas. If Shane wasn't mentally ready, if he got hurt again, it wouldn't end his career. But it might end hers. And seal his trade.

The lights went down, and a showgirl in a glittering, green leotard, feathers, and five-inch heels sang the national anthem. Allie focused on Shane. He stood in front of his net, shifting from foot to foot, staring down at the ice. In all his gear, he looked massive, but the nervous vibes he sent out made him seem small. Not good. As the song wound down, Shane tapped his stick against each goal post then dropped into a crouch and bounced a few times. Physically, he appeared fully healed. But the mental demons often decided a game.

The puck dropped, and play erupted at center ice. Hard not to watch it, but she kept her gaze on Shane. Even this close, she couldn't see much of his expression thanks to the ornate, black and green mask, but he looked like a compressed spring.

Not even a minute after the face-off, whistles blew, as a trip led to a fight on the other end of the ice. The Sinners ended up with two penalties, and the Sharks got one. Allie rubbed her forehead. She could almost read Shane's thoughts. A penalty kill so soon could be a dangerous thing—give the Sharks momentum.

Both clubs were fierce as they battled for the puck, but the Sinners did a good job of holding the other team at bay. Then a Shark intercepted a pass and got a breakaway, and Shane went one on one with the charging player.

It must have happened in seconds but felt like an eternity. Shane dropped down in butterfly position, his legs spread to each goal post, but at the last second, the Shark went high and shot the puck over Shane's left shoulder into the back of the net.

Allie closed her eyes as the arena echoed with boos. She looked back in time to see Shane smack the ice with his stick before he got up and skated back and forth behind his net, shaking his head. On one pass, he looked up, saw her, and stopped.

Damn. She tried to keep any kind of disappointment off her face as she nodded slowly once. Hopefully, it conveyed *Yes, I'm here. Yes, you can do this. Don't lose focus.* He gave no acknowledgment, just turned and took his place back in goal.

By the end of the first period, the Sharks scored once more. Allie stood aside as the Sinners filed past her to the locker room. When Shane passed, he glanced at her from the corner of his eye then looked away. He might not be mad at her, but he appeared furious at himself. Progress. At least he was beyond blaming the people around him. Still, the waves of shame, regret, and frustration rolling off him could have knocked her down. Those feelings were more than familiar from her playing days. Nealy went by, and the coach's tight posture guaranteed her team was about to get an earful.

The Sinners didn't look any better in the second period. They played like they didn't trust their goalie to back them up, which seemed to reinforce Shane's self-doubt. They worked so hard defensively that they remained scoreless going into the third, though the Sharks earned another point. In the last half of the final period, a couple more power plays afforded the Sharks two more goals. Five nothing.

Shane was the first off the ice and moved with speed and purpose to the locker room. Allie tried to say something, but he kept going, a locomotive of self-loathing that wouldn't be derailed. The rest of the team followed, heads bowed, and Nealy just about had steam coming out her ears.

Irrationally, guilt sat heavy on Allie's chest. *Just like Caleb.* Except he wasn't. Shane wasn't Caleb. He didn't get injured again. He just needed to get his game back. *And I will help you. Or die trying.* Knowing Shane, it could go either way.

Chapter Thirteen

Tuesday, May 7th

"Thanks, Allie."

"No problem, Teresa. Remember, no cramming for the LSATs in your bedroom anymore. Only go there when you're really tired and only to sleep."

"Right." The dancer smiled sheepishly. Even the best concealer MAC had to offer couldn't cover the dark circles under her eyes. "I guess insomnia's not a huge problem, but it's been affecting my dance."

"I'm glad you stopped by. Not being able to sleep affects your whole life, including studying for law school. And you're going to be a great lawyer."

"Thanks." Teresa headed for the door but paused. "You're an angel for doing this for us. Any time you want to come to practice, you're always welcome."

"It was pretty fun. I might stop by sometime. Let me know if things don't get better."

"Will do. Bye, Allie." As Teresa left, she nearly bumped into another girl on her way in.

This one didn't look familiar. Not a dancer. But there was something about her wide, whiskey brown eyes. "Hi. I'm Saralynn." Her million-watt, perfect smile clicked the pieces in place. "Reese's sister." So he hadn't been kidding about his family calling him Reese.

"It's nice to meet you. I'm—"

"Allie. I've heard a lot about you." An impish gleam accompanied the words.

Her stomach fell, first in dread, then in that skydiving kind of way at the possibility what he said wasn't all bad. "Oh. Well, what can I do for you?"

Saralynn took Shane's usual place on the couch opposite Allie's chair. "Officially, I'm here because Sinners PR wants to put together an article about the behind-the-scenes staff to run in the *Las Vegas Sun*. I'm really here because I wanted to meet the woman responsible for returning my brother to human form. After the injury, I didn't think it was possible."

Allie bit the inside of her lip and reined in an inappropriate laugh. Then the words sunk in, and happiness mixed with the regrets. She may have helped Shane on some level, but she'd still returned him to play before he was ready. And in about fifteen minutes, she'd have to deal with that. "You've noticed a difference in him?"

"Are you kidding? He went from grizzly bear to teddy bear in the couple weeks he was with you. You're a freakin' miracle worker. And he admitted he was wrong. Do you know how often *that* happens?"

"Not a lot."

Saralynn touched her finger to her nose. "I mean, before, he was the sweetest guy. Do anything for the people he cared about. This last year changed him. I know it was 'cause Carter retired." She picked at her perfect nails. "They were inseparable growing up. Always played together, traded together like they were a package deal. I know it's hard for Reese now, playing without him. But what are you gonna do, y'know? A concussion's a concussion. And Carter's so different with Jacey. So happy. I think Reese might be a little jealous."

All this time, and the way to get some insight into Shane was through his sister. Granted, most of it had already occurred to Allie, but she hadn't considered how Shane felt about Phlynn getting a new best friend. "He's been through a lot."

"Yeah. But you brought him back. And I wanted to say thanks."

"I'm not sure how much credit I can take for that—"

"All of it. Seriously. But a little heads-up … the Sinners won last night with Simkins in net. Reese rode the bench. So he might be a little rough around the edges when he gets here. He wouldn't talk to me last night, and he had a red-eye flight home from San Jose. I'm guessing he didn't sleep much."

"I know. I watched the game from home. I'll be gentle." Losing his first game back and then watching his team win without him. Even if he didn't blame her, there was a good chance she'd take the brunt of his frustration.

"Well, I should go. Oh, quick quote first. Dr. Kallen, how do you like working for the Sinners?"

"It's a great organization, and I'm proud to be part of the team."

"Fantastic." Saralynn flashed her pearly whites. "You've done this before." She stood and paused at the door. "I'm glad I got to meet you. Take care of my brother. I'll see you around." Halfway out, she glanced over her shoulder with a mysterious glint in her eyes. "I knew you'd be pretty."

Huh? Allie sat back and blinked in the absence of the glittery, bubbly whirlwind. No wonder the girl tired Shane out. He was lucky to have her for a sister though, whether he admitted it or not.

Speak of the devil. Shane slumped into her office, his head down, and a dark look on his face. "Did I just see Saralynn in here?"

"Yeah, you just missed her. She had to interview me for an article."

"Interview?" A flash of panic cut through his black mood.

"Relax. Nothing about you. Just how I like working for the team."

His shoulders dropped a notch, and he fell onto the couch, leaning his head back to stare at the ceiling.

Lovely. We're back to this.

• • •

Shane forced the tension from his frame. Okay, it was just for a team article, but seeing his sister coming out of Allie's office had nearly given him a stroke. He didn't need them comparing notes on the mess he'd made of his life. For once, it was a comfort knowing Allie could wait out his silence. He didn't feel like talking.

He could feel her gaze on him, calm and apparently blank, but he knew she was assessing. Sizing him up. Figuring him out. Soon enough she'd present her conclusion. *Good.* He needed someone to tell him what the hell was wrong. "I did what you said." It came out without his permission like word vomit.

"You talked to the guys?" Her voice was soft, careful. Like she thought he'd crack. Maybe she was right. Usually was.

He nodded.

"I think you psyched yourself out. You were nervous, and that first goal started a domino chain. I've been there." The gentleness in her voice and the way she looked at him soothed away some of his anxiety.

"Then you know the only way to fix that is to get a win, and the only way to do that is to keep playing. After Simkin's shutout last night, no way is Coach risking me again. And you know what? I don't blame her."

"Shane …" Allie leaned forward and curled her fingers into his palm, giving it a small squeeze. The contact sent an unexpected bolt of heat up his arm and through his body. He wanted to pull her close and make better use of the couch. The urge must have made it to his eyes, because she stilled, her gaze locked with his. She seemed surprised too but that gave way to acknowledgment of what they'd both been ignoring. The undeniable spark; the magnetic attraction.

She could always see into him, but he felt especially exposed. He didn't want to overstep bounds but couldn't keep his fingers from closing over hers and returning the squeeze.

Her throat worked as she tried to swallow. The tip of her tongue slid over her lips. When she spoke, her voice was lower, warmer. "You can get over this slump. You just have to forgive yourself for past mistakes and remember you're one of the best tenders in the league."

He smiled at how she clung to professionalism even now. He wasn't blind. The desire making him shift in his seat reflected in her deep, dark eyes. But she held back, and he didn't want to push. "You ever get tired of being right?"

Her tension eased a notch, and one corner of her mouth perked up, flashing a dimple. "Not so far, but I'll let you know. I have one more thought while I'm on a roll." She eased her fingers out of his, gave his hand a soft pat, then rested her forearms on her knees. At least she didn't retreat completely.

"Hit me."

"Did you talk to Phlynn?"

Should have seen that coming. He sighed and shook his head. "He's been busy. Hard to get in touch with." *And I really didn't want to.* "I thought it wouldn't matter because I understood how it affected my game. That's how it works, right? Face your problem, it goes away?"

"In this case, your problem is a person, and you need to face him. Literally. I could ask him to come here if you want."

"*No.* I mean … I'll talk to him. I just don't want an audience. Even if it's you."

Where did *that* come from? Ah, who was he kidding? This woman had taken over his thoughts. When he could think about anything besides playing. Her face haunted his dreams, and while some of them were R-rated, in most, they just hung out. Time to admit it. He had it bad for his therapist.

She stared at him with those dark brown eyes, a small smile curling her perfectly shaped lips. Allie didn't look like most women in Vegas. She beat them all, hands down. Nothing fake about her from hair color to personality. She didn't say anything, but she didn't need to. It was like she could read his thoughts, and he was getting pretty good at decoding hers. "What do I say?"

"To Phlynn?"

"Yeah. I can't blame him for his concussion. It's not his fault he can't play anymore. If I say I've been playing like shit because he's not there, I'll sound like a pansy, and he'll feel guilty even though he shouldn't. What good is it gonna do?"

"He wasn't just your captain. He was your best friend, too. You're missing him in more than one area of your life. You can macho that up however you want to, but you need to say it, and he needs to hear it. Trade or no trade, you need to salvage your friendship if you want to get back to your game."

He wanted to dismiss that and go back to burying anything he didn't want to deal with, but she was right. He rolled around her words and frowned. "Was my best friend?"

"Even best friends have rifts, and Phlynn not playing anymore is definitely part of it. But he's got a new person in his life who he confides in and spends most of his time with. In a way, she's taken your role."

"Jacey? You think I'm jealous of Jacey?"

"Aren't you? Just a little?"

"No. I'm glad Carter found Jacey. She brought out something in him I didn't think was possible. He's never been happier. And I'm happy for him."

"I know you are. But spouses by nature are each other's best friends. It's completely normal to feel a little left out."

Did he? Sure, Phlynn didn't come over to watch games anymore or go out clubbing with the team. They hadn't gone for a drink in a while. Hard to think about that or anything else when your game was in the toilet. Honestly, since he'd been seeing her, Allie filled that hole. He confided in her, joked with her. She was his therapist, but somehow had become more. Clearly. And he couldn't tell her.

But now that he *was* thinking about Phlynn … Shane leaned over, elbows on knees and face in hands. He knew what he had to do. At least where his ex-best friend was concerned.

Chapter Fourteen

Friday, May 10th

Shane sat on a plush bench by the pool, nursing his third beer. While tourists gaped at the atmosphere of Surrender—namely half-naked women and a giant silver anaconda hanging over the bar—he stared at nothing in particular, both eagerly anticipating and dreading his best friend's arrival. *You need to say it, and he needs to hear it.* Allie's words combined with a light buzz helped his resolve.

It had been a while, but nice to know Phlynn still knew where to find him. The man rounded the corner, drink in hand and dropped onto the bench next to him. "Damn, it's been too long."

"Yeah." Why did things feel so weird? This guy had been a brother to him his whole life. "I hate this, Phlynn. This isn't us. You can spare me the gay jokes, but I *miss* you, man. I miss locker room pranks, trash talking in practice, and going out for drinks after a game. Hanging out on the weekends. All of it." Once the confession began, it poured out, unstoppable. The beer might have helped. But it felt *good*. He'd held it in too long.

Phlynn stared at the pool and shook his head. "You think I don't miss it, too?" No anger, but an edge of frustration in his voice.

"I'm sure you miss playing. Hell, I missed it, and I've only been out for a month. I didn't mean to make it sound like that was your fault. I just meant—"

"I know. I missed it all, too."

Shane watched as drunken dancers grooved a little too close to the pool. "I feel like we should talk about football for a while. Earn back some man points."

Phlynn snorted. "Shut up, dude."

An enormous weight lifted, and things felt right again. "Allie said I had to come clean if I wanted to get back to my game. I think my play tanked this season because it wasn't the same without you. I'm not blaming you. This is all on me, and I know I can do better. I will. But I understand if you have to move me next season." So hard to get out, but there it was.

Phlynn stared at him with raised brows, quiet for a minute like he was trying to decide what to respond to first. "*Allie?*"

Of course he'd pick that. "That's what she said to call her."

"I'll bet she did." Phlynn smiled.

Déjà vu. Shane remembered a conversation word for word about a year ago, except he'd been teasing Carter for calling their new boss *Jacey*. "It's not like that." Was it?

"If anybody knows the words to that song, it's me."

"She's my doctor. If things were different, maybe. She's so smart, man. Scary smart. She figures you out before you even have a clue. She's always right, which you'd think might be annoying, but somehow it's not. She's funny and sweet and manages to put up with my ass. And okay, yeah, she has the best body I've ever seen." Was all that out loud? Time to stop drinking.

"You got it bad."

One dancer fell in the pool and pulled the other with her. Shane blinked then shrugged. "Doesn't matter. Nothin' I can do."

"She feel the same way?"

"Sometimes I think so. We have a connection, that's for sure. But she's so stoic, you know? She takes her job seriously."

"As general manager, I'm glad to hear that. As your best friend, I'm sorry. I've never seen you like this over a girl before."

"Yeah. She's just different. Special." God, he sounded like a Hallmark card. Two-beer limit from now on.

"She must be. I didn't know if anyone could get through to you, man. After the sprain, you were pretty far gone."

"I know. I'm sorry. It's like the worse I played, the more I panicked. Then after the injury, it was just anger. I took it out on everyone but myself, and I'm the only one who deserved it."

Phlynn went quiet, but he looked impressed. He bumped his shoulder against Shane's. "Behind you now. I know you can get your mojo back. I don't want to move you. I just need to see where we're at with the salary cap and the other unrestricted free agents when the season wraps."

Not a guarantee by any means, but it felt better knowing where Phlynn stood. "I hear you. So, you wanna get out of here and go watch game six, Caps and Bruins?"

"Thought you'd never ask."

• • •

Sunday, May 12th

Shane closed his eyes and tried to will away the nausea. He'd made it to Nealy's office door, and that was hard enough. No one else on the executive level today, but after practice, her majesty had requested a word. No idea what she wanted, but mandatory meetings were rarely good.

"In or out, Reese, don't be a tease." Her tiny voice came through the wall as if she could sense him hesitating.

He eased inside, closed the door and stood in front of her desk. "Wanted to see me, Coach?"

"Have a seat. And for God's sake, take that look off your face. I'm not going to demand your firstborn." Expressionless as usual, but a lighter, more teasing tone than normal.

A smile started at the corners of his mouth but didn't quite make it. He dropped into the chair opposite her and folded his hands over his stomach, thought better of it, and set them on the arm rests.

"Christ," she said in mock disgust and shook her head. She stared at him for a long minute. Was that compassion in her eyes? "I want you to start in game one."

He blinked. "What?" It sounded like she said she wanted him to start. But that wasn't possible. If it was a joke, her sense of humor had taken a wicked turn.

"You heard me. You've been through your bullshit. Gotten it out of your system. I liked what I saw in practice today. You're ready. Gotta get back in the saddle and lead this team to the finals. You're the franchise goaltender, and it's time to remind people of that."

Funny. Felt like she was reminding *him*. A warm and fuzzy moment with Nealy never seemed possible before, but damned if he didn't want to hug her now. "Thanks, Coach."

"You want to thank me? Win on Tuesday. Simkins had a comfort level with the Sharks, got in their heads. You have an undefeated record with the Blackhawks. This one's all you."

Instead of pressured, he felt raring to go. Tuesday couldn't come fast enough.

"All right, now get outta here. I gotta solidify the rest of the lineup."

"Yes, Coach." He grinned and couldn't stop, even as she shook her head watching him leave.

Chapter Fifteen

Tuesday, May 14th

Kevin Scott, left wing, sat on Allie's couch rolling a quarter over his knuckles back and forth. "I mean, I know it's eight years old, but I've had that strap since my juniors. I just don't play right without it."

It sounded exactly like what it was. Scott's lucky—and ancient—jock strap was falling apart and no longer usable. And his game was suffering. To most, it might sound ridiculous and gross. Okay, it was gross. But she understood the idea of a lucky object. Almost all athletes had them. "Forty-two's your number?" Not just jersey but lucky number. Another common thing.

Scott nodded.

"Pick out a new cup, one that feels right to you, and have forty-two sewn into the band."

"You think that'll work?" His copper brows arched up hopefully.

It will if you think it will. "I do." Absolute confidence in her expression and tone. "You've had that number since your juniors too, right?"

"Yeah. Yeah, I did." He smiled, showing perfect, white, and most likely fake teeth. "Thanks, Kally."

She smiled back. "I'm here to help."

He stood and lumbered to the door. "The guys were right. You're really good at this."

"Thanks." She resisted the urge to bounce in her chair. *They like me. They really like me.*

The door opened before Scott could reach for it, and Shane stood in the frame, his expression going from pleased to confused to wary in five seconds. "Scotty?"

"She's not just yours anymore, Reesey. Gotta share her now."

Shane looked less than happy about that. He probably wouldn't enjoy knowing she'd seen the whole team wander in at one point or another over the last few days. Her office was turning into Grand Central Station. Turned out the Hansel and Gretel trick worked. Tempt them with candy, and they come right in. Between the players and the dancers, her only down time had been at home—face down on her mattress before she'd had to get up and do it all over again.

When Scott left, Shane closed the door. "Miss Popular lately, huh?"

"I happen to be very charismatic and friendly."

That broke through any anger he might have had going, and he resumed the good mood he'd come in with. "Coach wants to start me tonight."

"That's awesome!" A shot of excitement and adrenaline jolted through her as if she'd be the one out there.

He beamed in response. "She must have faith in me."

"I do too. And so should you." She poked him in the chest.

He looked down at her playfully. "Well. Guess I have to listen to the miracle worker."

"I didn't work any miracles. I just helped you get out of your own way."

"Yeah. You really did." His gaze turned serious, and the air thickened to a honey consistency. As he leaned forward, she artfully slid around the coffee table, heart pounding, and fell into her wingback chair, making it look nonchalant. "So, you excited for tonight?" If she didn't acknowledge the flirting, it wasn't official.

He looked down, but a puff of breath belied his laugh. At least he didn't take offense to her deflection. But he also didn't seem to take it seriously. Shane dropped onto his usual place on the couch.

"Sort of. You really think I'll be okay? I talked to Phlynn. We're good now."

The switch of topics loosened her posture. "That's great. I think that was the only thing holding you back. You know you can trust your team as it is. They're strong, and now you are too."

He nodded, staring unfocused at the bookcase on the opposite wall.

"What did Phlynn say?"

Shane blinked and came back to her. "We had an embarrassing heart-to-heart. He said he missed playing with me too. Wants to hang out more. Doesn't want to trade me if he can afford to keep me."

"That's good and I'm sure a weight lifted. Would you negotiate to stay in Vegas?" She knew he would but didn't want him to feel like she knew everything about him. Guys didn't like to think they were predictable, even athletes with strict routines and habits.

"I would. I want to stay here. I like this team and the city, and …" His gaze flickered over her face then away. "And it's not about money. I have more than I'll ever need." Hard for her to imagine what that was like, but he clearly meant it. "I never thought adult Disneyland could feel like home, but it does."

"It does, doesn't it? There's something nice about feeling like you can go anywhere in the world in fifteen minutes." And leave the bright lights behind for her cute, little neighborhood just as fast. Best of both worlds.

Shane grinned. "It sucked you in, too."

"Guilty." And he would as well if she didn't watch it. There was something between them. It was undeniable, but she could ignore it. Good thing he'd be getting back on the ice and the constant temptation would go with him. A dose of regret and shame piggybacked her intense attraction even though he appeared to feel the same way.

His gaze went from flirty to thoughtful. "So you really believe I'll be okay tonight?" Fear turned even the most logical people into broken records. At least it broke her train of thought.

"I think you will be if you stop asking that question and start telling yourself you're going to rock tonight."

Ah, the dimple. It returned with a vengeance and a smile that made her glad she was already sitting down.

"You gonna be there?"

"Oh, I have a feeling Nealy will want me front and center again. Is that okay?"

"I can deal with that." The gleam in his dark amber eyes showed just how much of an understatement that was. Her heart stutter-stepped, and she pressed her moist palms against the fabric of the armrests. *Get a grip.* Why was she getting schoolgirl excited about this unattainable train wreck? Maybe because the wreck reminded her so much of herself.

"Earth to Allie." He poked her pump with one of his Adidas sandals. He wore them with white socks rolled up to his knees. It might look strange to outsiders, but she'd committed the same fashion crime in her playing days. Only her socks were tie-dye.

"Sorry. It's been a long couple days."

"So I hear. The whole team coming in now?"

Unexpected pleasure sparked inside at the twinge of jealousy in his voice. "Just about."

"Yeah, well I saw you first." Staking claim. Joking, but an undercurrent of truth ran just beneath.

"Against your will." He started to protest, and she held up a hand. "It's okay. Besides, you've graduated. You don't need to see me anymore."

"That's not great incentive to play well tonight." His smile was teasing, and her heart—traitorous, irrational muscle—cartwheeled.

"No? How about another championship ring and a guaranteed stay in Vegas?" She kept her tone light to take some of the sting out of that bald truth, but he had to stay focused. They both did.

His face went solemn, and after a minute, he nodded.

It was stupid to feel disappointed for getting the reaction she'd wanted from him, so she pushed it down. "Now go get some rest. You're going to kick all kinds of ass tonight."

The light returned to his eyes. Before she knew what was happening, he stood, leaned down, and brushed his lips whisper-soft against her forehead. Gentle and sweet. Not usual patient behavior, but it didn't cross a solid line either. "Thanks again, Allie. For everything. See you tonight?" Even with all of her reassurances, he still looked nervous about returning to the net.

"I'll be there."

Chapter Sixteen

Game One of the Conference Finals. Not like elimination was on the line, but that didn't mean Shane wasn't bomb-defusal tense when he pushed into the locker room. The guys lifted their heads from dressing and taping to greet him with smiles and nods, and he returned the gesture on autopilot.

"Yo, Reese. Looks like you got a secret admirer." Kevin Scott tilted his head toward a clear plastic baggie closed with a silver twist-tie sitting in front of his locker. "What are those? Look like rabbit turds."

Shane frowned and picked up the baggie for closer inspection. Chocolate-covered gummy bears. There was an un-signed note taped to the bottom.

I'd tell you to break a leg, but you might actually do it. Try these instead.

He couldn't help a big, dumb smile that made his cheeks hurt. "Allie."

"Allie? You mean Kally? Why are you teacher's pet? How come she didn't bring enough for the whole class?"

"Shut up, Scotty. They're for good luck."

The left wing's ginger eyebrows rose as he traded his mocking expression for an earnest one. "Can I have some?"

Seeing Scotty serious about anything threw Shane for a loop. The man had been his semi-playful tormentor over the last few months. Part of Shane wanted to flip him off and down the whole bag right there. But it had cost Scotty a lot to ask, and if he could help a teammate, shouldn't he? Not that the gummy bears actually had super powers. Still, it couldn't hurt. "Sure." He unwound the tie and shook a few into Scotty's hand.

"Thanks, man."

"No problem." Shane tossed a few in his own mouth then set the bag on a shelf in his locker. Sweet and fruity, they proved a good distraction as he slipped out of his suit and into his gear. The mindless mechanics of the process helped calm him down, and by the time he laced up his skates and slipped his jersey over his head, he was ready to get out there.

Jacey came in and got the guys riled up, hooting and hollering. He even joined in this time. When she left, Coach and Cole stood opposite each other at the tunnel entrance and clapped players on the back as they filed past. Cole gave his shoulder a squeeze when he went by and barked, "Let's go, Reesey!" Nothing patronizing about it, just heartfelt excitement and support. His adrenaline kicked up a notch, and he jogged the rest of the way, jumping onto the ice with purpose.

Lights flashed around the arena, and pre-game music all but drowned out the announcer reciting the starting lineup. The cheers were deafening, but even those were muted by his pounding heart. He glided side to side in short, quick movements, etching traction marks in his crease. Just a couple seconds until puck drop. Where was Allie?

Movement registered in the corner of his vision. His good luck charm hustled down the tunnel and stood by the glass, strands of dark hair falling from her ponytail to frame her beautiful face. She grinned and gave him a thumbs-up. His heart swelled to twice the size, and more than ever he wanted to skate over there and kiss her until they had to come up for air. Now was not the time; but soon.

As a renowned lounge singer belted out the anthem, he faced the flag but closed his eyes and shifted foot to foot. On the last note, he knocked the blade of his stick against one goal post then the other before hopping into a puck-ready crouch.

• • •

Being on the sidelines before a game versus being out there with the team made Allie's nerves ten times worse. She popped a couple gummy bears in her mouth and chewed hard as the puck dropped. A flurry of action broke out, and play rushed toward the Sinners' zone. Of course. No easing into the game for Shane and no easing the bile production in her stomach. She popped an antacid and choked down the minty, chalky substance.

Shane just about fell over to make the first save, and his sloppiness meant a big rebound. The resulting shot pinged off the crossbar and sent the puck into the corner. He scrambled to his feet and shook his head as if to clear the fog. The rest of the first period continued in the same haphazard, frenzied manner. When he lumbered past her to the locker room, he didn't look up from his skates. *Don't do it. Don't fall into the trap.* It could be all too easy for a goalie to let an iffy opening determine the rest of the game, but he seemed better than the last time. Tonight he'd begun with a smile and a sense of ease he'd been missing since last season, if the tapes had shown her anything. A verbal smack upside the head from Nealy, and he should be okay.

After Sinbad, the mascot devil, shot t-shirts into the audience with the help of Lady Sinners, the lights lowered for the period break, and Zambonis glided silently around the rink, laying down fresh ice. There was something soothing, almost meditative about it. As high-energy, high-stress as the game could be, the Zen-like intermissions acted as a good counterbalance.

Just as serenity set in, the team filed past her; determination on their faces and sweat stink emanating through their gear. When Shane went by, she swatted his shoulder. He glanced at her, blank at first, then the corner of his mouth turned up in an acknowledgement that pierced her professional armor. Before she could think too much on that, Nealy brought up the rear and touched her elbow.

"What's your diagnosis?"

"Better than it looks. First period was a little shaky, but I could see his confidence coming back. I think it'll only get better from here."

"Agreed. Glad we're on the same page. Let's just hope Reese keeps up with us." Nealy's tone said she had every confidence he would. She stepped onto the ice in her kitten heels, and Dylan Cole, who'd been hanging back, offered an arm to escort their coach to the team bench. Oddly adorable, especially because Dylan's tight posture belied his respect, awe, and fear of the tiny woman he ushered. Allie watched for a minute then turned her focus on Shane.

Whatever Nealy said to him couldn't have been too harsh because he appeared loose-limbed and relaxed. He rolled his neck—not easy with the big mask—and dug his blades into the ice inside his crease, all the while a distant but focused look in his dark eyes. She knew "the zone" when she saw it, and thank God he'd found his way back. It could be an elusive thing, especially after an injury.

The Sinners didn't score in the second period, but neither did the Blackhawks. By the third period, Shane was flawless, and he knew it; judging by the giant grin every time he made a save to the roar of the crowd. As the seconds wound down in the last minute, the Sinners played with the blatant confidence granted by the two-goal lead they'd gained, and when the final buzzer sounded, the whole team rushed their goalie to envelop him in hugs and touch their helmets to his.

Even immersed in the commotion, all she could see was the euphoria and triumphant relief on Shane's face. Those emotions filled her, too, but not with pride, at least not fully. This wasn't the same as past professional successes. It meant something more. *He* meant something more.

She pulled her gaze away from the ice and hurried down the tunnel and through the locker room before the team followed. Safe in her office, she leaned against the door and closed her eyes.

• • •

Shane ambled down the tunnel to the locker room, half-paying attention to his excited teammates bumping his shoulder, patting his mask, and barking, "Fuckin' awesome!" Their support meant a lot, but right now, something else meant more. He shed his gear in front of his locker. As soon as he got down to athletic shorts and a t-shirt, he slipped into the quiet hallway.

Adrenaline and emotion carried him to Allie's office, and when he opened the door, she stumbled forward as if she'd been leaning against it.

"Shane?" A mix of confusion, happiness, and something like regret played on her face. "You were amazing out there. You—"

He scooped her up and swung her around. She gasped and laughed, holding onto his shoulders, and it felt even better than the win. He smiled so hard his cheeks hurt, and when he set her down, he backed her against the door and kissed her. Her lips were soft, warm, and moist. She tasted like cherries, and the citrus-vanilla of her perfume filled his head. Her body stiffened, but she didn't pull back or push him away. Because his palms rested against her neck, he could feel her pulse trying to outpace a German train. He slid his thumbs lightly along her cheekbones and nudged her nose with his. When their foreheads touched, her lashes fluttered, and her breath rushed warm against his lips. She met his gaze and whispered, "Shane …"

Since peewee hockey, no one had called him anything but Reese at his own request, but God, he couldn't get enough of the sound of his name from her mouth. In the next second the enormity of what he'd done sunk in, and he took a step back, eyes wide as he tried to get his emotional bearings. "Allie. I'm sorry. I didn't mean—I was so caught up … but I crossed a line. Even though I guess I'm officially not your patient anymore."

The shock on her face couldn't hide a trace of pleasure. Her voice came out low and unsteady. "It's all right. You were just carried away. You're not my patient now, but you might be in the future, so … we probably shouldn't make a habit of it." She smiled the way she did when she wanted to deflect, but the look in her eyes said she wasn't so sure.

"Yeah." But neither moved. He couldn't look away. How were they supposed to pretend this didn't exist? That it wasn't important? Apparently, he was pretty good at self-deception, but even with his exceptional skill in denial, he couldn't wrap his mind around treating Allie like one of the guys.

She angled back and set a hand on the doorknob. "You should go celebrate with your team. That was some win."

Pride spread in his chest, and the locker room did beckon, but even accolades for his impressive performance couldn't outmatch how good it felt just being in the same room with her. It took physical effort to stride past when she held open the door. He paused in the hallway, hating the thought that he wouldn't really have time with her anymore. "I'll see you around, okay?"

"I'll be here." She smiled, but the shade of sadness in her eyes said it hurt her too.

A new appreciation dawned on him for what his best friend went through the past year, but there didn't seem to be a light at the end of this tunnel.

Chapter Seventeen

Thursday, May 16th

"Thanks for doing this." Allie lay stretched out on the sofa in her office, one arm dangling over the side and the other resting over her face so that her eyelashes brushed against the crook of her elbow. Shane's session time was now painfully empty, and this seemed like the perfect filler.

Mac sat in the "doctor chair," legs crossed, holding her chin in one hand thoughtfully. "What are friends for? Even the best therapists can't diagnose themselves."

"Ugh. I don't need *diagnosed*. I need to spill my guts to a girlfriend because telling anyone else would get me fired."

"Ooo, intrigue. Continue."

Allie opened one eye to glare. "That's not incredibly supportive."

Mac shrugged unapologetically. "You're right. I don't have your training. Now spill."

Allie blew out a long breath. As much as her thoughts had been pin-balling furiously around her brain for the last day and a half, now that the time had come to expunge, it was surprisingly hard.

"This is about Shane," Mac guessed.

She lifted the arm off her face and blinked.

"I knew it! You like him, don't you?"

"It's worse than that." Allie squeezed her eyes closed.

"You slept with him."

Allie sat up on one elbow and gaped. "No!"

"Well, you should. 'Cause *damn*."

"*Mac*."

"Sorry." Her friend smiled sheepishly. "Blame the pregnancy hormones. Well, what is it then?"

Allie laid back and plopped a pillow over her face, mumbling her answer. It was too horrible to say without a fluffy filter.

"Remove that right now or I will beat you to death with it." Mac sounded about as serious as she ever did, so heeding that warning was the only option.

She put the pillow back but kept her eyes firmly shut. "He kissed me."

"And?"

"I let him." Guilt laced those three words, and was well-deserved if Mac's responding silence was any indicator. Her stomach sank, and shame threatened to crush her. Summoning a scrap of bravery, she peeked at her friend. "Well?"

Mac pressed her lips together and sighed. Finally, she said, "Explain to me the problem part?"

Seriously? Allie sat up, hands squeezing her knees as she tried to keep her voice down. Even in a basement office with cement walls, you couldn't be too careful. "How about the part where I'm the world's worst therapist because I kissed a patient?"

"You said he kissed you. Did you kiss back?"

"Well, no. But I didn't push him away either."

"Did you like it?"

She felt again the soft, sweet burn of his lips, his rough, callused palms lightly caressing her neck, his hard body leaning into her, promising so much more. "That's … not the point."

"So that's a yes."

Allie pointed to her own face. "Notice the exasperation."

Mac giggled. Actually giggled. "I'm sorry. I'm sorry, Kally. I understand what you're saying, and I know it could potentially be a big deal, but right now it's just a kiss from a *former* patient. Otherwise he'd be here right now instead of me. He'd just won his first game after the injury, and it sounds like a heat of the moment thing. You won't be seeing him anymore, so you could just let it go if that's what you want."

Allie recognized verbal bait when she heard it. Normally she was the one dishing it out. "But you don't think that's what I want."

"*You* don't think that's what you want, or you wouldn't be coming to me for advice. Let's face it. I got lucky with David. I was a relationship wrecking ball in college, and we both know it."

Hard to refute that. Mac had been a party girl and left more than a string of broken hearts in her wake. But she seemed happy now, so she must have figured it out at some point. It was more than Allie could claim.

"Even though he's not my patient now, he could be in the future, and I wouldn't be able to treat him. And then I'd have to explain why. It just feels wrong."

"But he doesn't."

She wanted to deny that, but no one had ever been able to read her better than her college roommate, so it wouldn't make a difference. "No. He doesn't. He feels …" Perfect. Incredibly right. "If I had met him any other way, *I* would have asked *him* out by now."

"Trust me, that wouldn't have been necessary."

Allie raised a brow.

"When he came to me, Kally, you should have seen him. Tail between his legs—full-out desperate because he raised his voice at you. Begging me to help him find a way to make it right. He wanted to make it personal so it would mean something. Even putting the hot bod aside, this one has keeper written all over him. Pun intended."

"But I *can't* keep him. I need this job. And for the first time, I feel needed. The dancers depend on me, and the guys are just starting to come around and open up. I can really help here, and that's all I've wanted since my surgery. I'm not going to throw that away for a guy."

"Even if he's *the* guy?"

"Mac."

"Kally. You and I never really bought into the gushy love stuff, but then I found David, and I gotta say, I get it now. Me, of all people. And I think Reese might be your David."

"You're basing this on him asking you my favorite candy?"

"I'm basing this on the candy thing, the date at my complex, and the last twenty minutes of seeing my friend miserable because an amazing guy kissed her and she can't do anything about it."

"That wasn't a date. He blackmailed me into letting him tag along."

Mac scrunched her face. "I call bullshit. Alexandra Kallen doesn't let anyone tell her what to do."

It was impossible to counter the truth.

"Kally, you wouldn't be so torn up if you didn't really care about this guy. Your big, rational brain is trying to steamroll your heart, and this," Mac gestured to herself in the therapist chair and Allie on the couch, "this is your heart fighting back. Who are you going to listen to?"

The answer should be obvious. Problem was, before now, it wouldn't even be a question.

• • •

5:00 P.M.

Shane had made it about forty-three hours, but if he didn't do something now, he'd get the shakes and sweat bullets. Staying away from Allie proved almost impossible, especially when he knew she was just down the hall. His gut kept saying *What's stopping you? Go.* Then his brain would come back with *And then what? Declare your undefined feelings and get her fired?* Until now, his brain had won, but an athlete's gut wouldn't be denied for long. He had only a half-cooked plan for what he'd do once he got there, but it wasn't a choice anymore.

Facing her door, he reached for the knob, hesitated, and knocked.

"Come in."

He eased it open, his pulse pounding in his ears. "Hey."

She'd been taking notes at her desk, and when she looked up, pleasant shock took over her face, replaced quickly with a more tempered, formal, friendly curiosity. "Hey, what brings you by? I fixed you."

In more ways than she'd ever know. "Yeah. You did. Um …" Blank. What now? *I just wanted to see you* might be the truth, but it had a pathetic ring to it, and what if she didn't want to see him? Oh right, the half-cooked plan. "Saralynn has a date tonight. Some guy she met at a club last weekend. I don't want to be the overbearing brother, and she wouldn't go for a chaperone, but I really don't want her out by herself with a guy she doesn't know. So I'm here for a favor. The only deal I could strike was a double date."

Allies eyes widened, and her lips parted slightly.

He wanted to lean over the desk and kiss her again, but that wasn't a good long-term plan. "Not that it would really be a date. For us I mean. You'd just be helping me keep an eye on Saralynn. Plus, you're a good judge of people. You can do your *Mentalist* thing and see if this guy's good enough."

She tilted her head, and a wave of dark brown hair fell over her shoulder. "Could any guy ever be good enough?"

For his baby sister? Absolutely not. "Well, see, that's why I need you. I might be a little biased."

"You? Never."

"Okay, okay. Please?"

She sat back, and the turning mental gears showed in her pursed lips and squinting eyes. She wasn't looking for an excuse. Allie didn't do that. Straight shooting was one of her most attractive qualities. No, she'd be looking at the proposal from every possible angle, weighing the cost-benefit analysis. "Okay."

"Okay?" She really just agreed? It couldn't be that easy.

"Sure. Why not? I don't have anything else to do, and I know it won't be a late night because you've got a game tomorrow, and you're way too afraid of Nealy to miss the morning skate."

His mouth fell open, but a defending remark died in his throat.

Allie waved off his reaction. "It's okay. If she were my coach, she'd scare me too. Honestly, she still kind of does."

Some of his discomfort faded. If Nealy made *Allie* nervous, that was vindication enough. "Great. So, seven o'clock at Red Rock Lanes. Do you want me to pick you up, or …?"

"I'll meet you there. I have some errands to run after work."

"Okay." It was crazy to feel disappointed, but it made sense she'd keep her boundaries. She'd agreed; that was a start. And he never had a problem putting work in for something he wanted. "Well, I'll see you then."

"See you then." Her casual cool had him feeling even more awkward. Few times in his life did he feel like the nerd asking out the cheerleader, but that seemed accurate at the moment. She kept his ego in check. He'd give her that.

Chapter Eighteen

Allie stared at the glowing sign that read Red Rock Lanes. Why did she agree to this? It was clearly a bad idea. Her responsible therapist side had no doubt about the right thing to do. Unfortunately, the hopeful romantic she tried to keep hidden was the one holding the car keys. What did Mac say? This was her heart fighting back. She blew out a sigh. Might as well get it over with.

The bowling alley was jumping for a Thursday night, but then again, Las Vegas was one endless weekend. Shane stepped into view by the front desk and waved her over. He'd erased the stubble from his chin and traded the t-shirt and shorts from practice for dark-wash jeans and a white button-down shirt with the sleeves rolled to the elbow. It glowed under the neon lights, and when he smiled, his teeth had the same effect, kind of Cheshire Cat-like. He lifted his voice over the music and sea of other voices. "What size shoes do you wear?"

"Eight." Oops. Was he going to pay? She angled closer to protest but stopped. True, it might be too much like a date if he paid, but he made more in a day than she did in a month, and the effort to be heard over the ruckus wasn't worth preserving a small boundary. He'd invited her out as a friend. He could pay ten bucks for her to bowl. But that was the last concession. If she kept it up, she might reason herself into kissing him again. *Wow, that kiss.*

Before she could replay it for the hundredth time, she focused instead on Saralynn. The younger Reese had opted for a billowy, hot pink, chiffon blouse, dark skinny jeans and silver gladiator sandals. Her long, light brown hair was pulled back in a ponytail.

For most women, it was a typical first date outfit. For Saralynn, it didn't exactly add up. Way too much coverage, and no way Shane had any say in what his sister wore. Curious.

Size eight saddle shoes appeared in Allie's field of vision, and she took them from Shane's outstretched hand. "Thanks."

His dimples winked at her.

Oh boy. Time to think of anything else. As the group walked toward their lane, she took the opportunity to scope out Saralynn's mystery date. Tall and lean, clean cut with hipster glasses and a button-down plaid shirt. Pants so tight they looked like leggings and Converse sneakers. She might not know Saralynn *that* well, but this guy didn't seem like her type. When they all sat on the horseshoe bench by their lane to switch out their shoes, Hipster lifted his head and smiled politely. "Hi, I'm Ted."

"Allie. Nice to meet you." She glanced at Saralynn, whose entire attention remained on her nails.

"We ready to get started or what?" Saralynn hopped up to the monitor and touched the screen to begin their game. Her name was at the top, so she selected a neon orange ball, approached the line with a wobble, and rolled the ball right into the gutter. Twice. "Oops. You're up, Ned."

The corners of Ted's eyes crinkled, but he didn't correct her. Apparently, Saralynn's million-watt grin took the sting out of forgetting his name. He ambled up, chose a green ball, and tip-toed to the line.

"So what do you think?" Shane's husky voice rumbled in her ear, and she jumped.

How did he get so close? His shoulder brushed hers, and if she turned her head, they'd be nose to nose. She pressed her lips together and stared down at her lap. "I think she's going to eat poor 'Ned' alive."

Shane laughed deep and throaty, and the sound shot a tingle down her spine. This close, the citrus and musk of his cologne just about short-circuited her brain. From the corner of her eye, she saw the pulse point at his neck and struggled not to lean in and kiss it.

Holy self-control. She slid over half a foot for some space and closed her eyes for a second.

"You're up, Allie," Ted called as he sauntered back to the bench. According to the scoreboard, he'd picked up an impressive spare that she'd missed entirely. And so had Saralynn, who didn't look up from her phone as Ted sat hip to hip with her.

Allie bit her lip and picked a purple ball. Ten pounds. She tested the weight in her hand. Heavy but not overly. She made a not-so-graceful approach, but she drew her arm back and aimed as straight as possible. She shifted from foot to foot as it rolled along, and when all of the pins went down, she threw her arms in the air and danced in a circle. "Whoo!"

"And I had you pegged for a gracious winner," Shane said. He looked happier than she'd ever seen him, even when he'd won that first game back. Her heart hiccupped.

He held his hand up for a high-five in passing, and she obliged. His fingers curled around hers briefly in a small squeeze. To observers, they were little, casual gestures. Platonic. But she knew better. She took a seat and tried to look anywhere except his butt as he leaned over and chose a ball, but the fit of his jeans demanded attention. *I am in so much trouble.*

In her peripheral vision, Ted slid his arm along the back of the bench and theoretically around Saralynn's shoulders, except the younger Reese deftly pivoted to her feet. "Anyone need a drink?"

"I got it, babe." Smitten, Ted jumped up then raised eyebrows at Allie.

"Just a water, thanks."

"You got it. And a beer for the bro." Ted shuffled off toward the bar.

When Saralynn reclaimed her seat, Allie sat beside her as Shane took his first roll. "You don't like that guy."

"Hmm?" Saralynn went wide-eyed and innocent.

"Save it. Your neckline is touching your neck, your hair is up, and your date shoes were flat. Every time he gets closer, you back away but keep it subtle except when Shane is looking, and then you're all over the guy. Oh, and you forgot his name."

"But Ned is—"

"Ted. So if you're not really into Ted, this date was to get back at your brother for trying to control your life?"

Saralynn's doe façade cracked, and her lips quirked to the side, calculating. "I'm not trying to get back at my brother. That's a fun side effect. I'm trying to help him."

Now things started making sense. "So this has nothing to do with Ted or revenge and was just a trap for us?"

Mischief lit Saralynn's eyes. "If you mean like *The Parent Trap*, then yes. And there's a little revenge mixed in. Two birds."

Allie's temples throbbed, and she squeezed her eyes closed. "We're just friends. He was my patient. I can't date him. We're not—"

"Totally into each other? C'mon, Doc, even I can see that. You check each other out constantly. There's a definite vibe."

He checked her out? *Not important.* Who else could have seen? Panic put a brick in her stomach as she imagined other players—Nealy, Phlynn, or even Jacey—noticing the apparently obvious connection she had with their goalie. Therapists prided themselves on not being as emotionally transparent as the rest of the populous. So it seemed Shane wasn't the only one skilled in self-deception.

When in doubt, deflect. "Your brother and I will figure out what we are without help, as well-intentioned as it might be. Meanwhile, Ted really likes you, so if you're not interested, be honest. And gentle." Because Shane's sister had a knack for the straightforward.

Saralynn rolled her eyes. "Yes, Mom. By the way, how do you know he likes—"

"He didn't ask what you wanted to drink, so he already knew. Which means he remembered from the other night. And people only make an effort to remember what's important to them." The "Mom" comment got under her skin, but she needed to stay on track.

The snark drained out of Saralynn's expression, replaced with what looked like thoughtful consideration. *Good.* Maybe Ted had a chance.

"Y'know, I think I'll go see if he needs help carrying drinks."

That called for a mental pat on the back. Sometimes people could surprise you, and not always negatively. As Saralynn headed for the bar, she glanced over her shoulder, looking between Shane and Allie, then winked and disappeared into the crowd, leaving them alone.

Crap. Had again.

Shane sat beside her after picking up a spare and looked around. "What'd I miss?"

"My arms are too short to box with Saralynn."

"Huh?"

"Your sister set us up. She's not on the real date. We are."

"But she was all over that guy."

"When you were looking. Poor Ted was a prop. Although, I may have been able to change her mind about that, but it's hard to tell. The girl's got game."

He studied her face, a hint of nervousness in his gaze. "Are you mad?"

She should be annoyed, but nope, not even a little bit. That couldn't be good. "I can tell you didn't know anything about it, so no. Are you mad?"

"That my baby sister still knows how to get me to do exactly what she wants, hell yes. And I didn't even realize it this time, so she's getting better. That's scary."

"What about why she did it?"

His gaze dropped from her face to the floor before he stared at the score monitor. "I know what I should say. But the truth is I'm not mad or sorry. I'd have asked you out myself if I could have worked up the guts."

Her mouth went dry. What had she expected by poking and prodding? It was disconcerting that her brain no longer had full control of her tongue. She'd asked, and he was saying the words she knew he would. Part of her had wanted to hear them. Now what? "Shane ..."

"I never would have chosen to fall for my therapist, but there's something here, Allie. And there's no point in pretending otherwise now. You're not treating me. You're not liable for me. I swear to God I'll never hit another teammate or damage team property. Hell, I won't even knock my stick against the goal post after I miss one if it means you'll give me a chance."

The full-on eye contact and seriousness of his expression hit the words home even harder. No deflecting this time. He was being honest. So could she. He deserved that much. "It's completely unprofessional, but I like you too. If we had met any other way, it would be different. You know how I sometimes know you better than you know yourself? That's only part training. The other part is I know *me*, and you and I are so alike it's spooky."

The corner of his mouth curled up. "So it scares you, too?"

"To death. But there's nothing we can do. Even if I never treat you again, I could lose my job if anyone found out. And ... I'd feel like I was taking advantage of you. I know it doesn't seem like it, but there's a thing called transference when a patient develops feelings for a doctor because—"

He cupped a hand around her neck and cut off further explanation with his mouth over hers. Possessive, confident, passionate. The tip of his tongue teased her lips, and her logic train jumped the rails. She gave in without a thought, surrendered to the moment, and kissed him back. Reckless, but she tingled head to toe with forbidden excitement. She *wanted* him, and he very clearly wanted her.

He broke the kiss but barely, and his breath hitched as he tried to catch it. "You're not taking advantage. You're not breaking a trust with me or anyone else. Something that feels this right can't possibly be wrong."

She smiled as she struggled to wade out of the desire haze. "Of course it can. That's the danger of temptation."

His hand slid from her neck so he could thread his fingers through hers. "If we're the same, then you're not the kind of person who can live with regret. I can't. And I have a feeling this would be a big one."

How did he do it? Get to the bare truth so easily? Well, turnabout was fair play. If she could see inside him, it only made sense he'd be able to do the same to her. No, she and regret weren't on speaking terms. In fact, she'd fought her whole life to make up for every regret possible. Her career-ending injury, and then Caleb's. The penance for those things had been clear, but if she walked away from Shane, could she ever fix it?

"C'mon, Allie. One date. A real one. And if you still don't think it's worth it, we'll go on with our lives the way they are—no harm, no penalty."

Ohh, that sounded tempting. Just one date. Her resolve crumbled around the edges. "Isn't it 'no harm, no foul'?"

He lifted his brows. "You think you're dating a basketball player?"

"What was I thinking? And I'm not *dating* you. One date. One."

"Whatever you say." His tone said he was confident of multiple repeats.

She narrowed her eyes in playful suspicion then stuck her tongue out at him. "Well, what about this date? We can't exactly finish the game without the two other bowlers. Saralynn's up, and I don't think she's coming back."

"Because she wants to spend the night with Ted?"

"Because she wants you to spend the night with me."

He looked like a little boy with the keys to Toys R Us, and she laughed. "Ah, ah. You think I'm that easy?"

The strobe light lit his amber eyes and so did the drive she usually saw when he was on the ice. "I know you're not, but I've always loved a challenge."

No answer to that, really. So did she. Though, this might be one she was willing to lose.

"And in answer to your first question, we can play the rest of the game ourselves. You be you and Saralynn, I'll be me and Ted. Girls against guys."

"I feel like there's a multiple personalities joke in there, but I can't quite find it."

He took her hand and kissed her knuckles. "And for our real date, how's Saturday night? I'll cook you dinner."

"At your place? And give Saralynn another chance to 'help'? How about you cook and bring it over my house?"

"Huh. You may have a point. Okay, your place it is. Six o'clock?"

"Deal." It just popped out, no chance to over-think. Her brain was definitely taking the backseat these days.

Chapter Nineteen

Saturday, May 18th

Never being home had its perks. Like when company came, there wasn't much cleaning to do. Allie zipped around her little house, sliding a dust rag over countertops and any other surface that looked like it needed it. Top to bottom, that took twenty minutes. At five-thirty she traded sweatpants and her Lady Sinners tank top for dark jeans, a purple, frilly, short-sleeved blouse, and wedge sandals. She shook her hair out of a ponytail and brushed it straight, then swiped on some lip gloss. Good to go.

Dave Matthews crooned from the hidden stereo speakers while she set two places at the kitchen table. These mechanical things kept her mind off the real issue—she was *dating* a patient. No. Ex-patient. And one date didn't qualify as dating. Hearing that from a client, she'd call it denial. For now, she'd call it a moral loophole.

Her cell phone rang, and her heart jumped into action. Was he having second thoughts? Relief and disappointment shared space in her head until she answered and Mac's voice burst onto the line.

"Is he there yet? What's he wearing? You changed out of the sweats, right?"

"Jesus, Mac, you scared me. No, he's not here yet, and yes, I changed out of the sweats."

"Hey, I know you. I had to check."

"I know how to date."

Her friend snickered. "You *knew* how to date. After Stanford, your lover was named Grad School, and the dress code's different."

Allie tipped her head back and took a slow breath. "I promise. I'm so girly you'd roll your eyes."

"Good. I expect full details the minute he leaves, and I'm up late. I'm also up early if the date should last until breakfast."

"Mac!"

"Hey, if you're so determined to make it just one date, you might as well get the full experience."

Allie rubbed her forehead. "I will talk to you sometime in the undetermined future when I have forgiven you."

"You love me."

"Bye, Mac." She dropped her phone back in her shoulder bag just before a car pulled into the driveway.

• • •

Shane parked in the short, narrow driveway and stared at the butter-yellow dollhouse in front of him. *Cute* was the first word that came to mind. It didn't entirely jive with the sleek, sporty, sexy image he had of Allie, but something about it fit just right. Cozy. Comfortable. A refreshing piece of the Midwest just outside of Vegas, not unlike Allie herself. The entire neighborhood had that vibe, and it felt like his home back East. Pleasant Valley Sunday on a Saturday night.

His big Explorer looked a little out of place amid the street of small sedans, but no one seemed to notice. He collected the Tupperware containers from the passenger seat along with the bottle of wine and hip-checked the door closed.

Allie must have heard him coming because she appeared and waved him inside before he'd taken two steps away from his car. He almost stumbled staring at her while trying to navigate her porch. Date Allie wasn't a big stretch from Work Allie except … girlier? Sexier?

She took a couple containers off the top of the pile in his arms, easing his load. "Wow. You take dinner seriously. You made all this?"

"I did. My mom's a great cook. Raised me right. I don't do this all the time, but it seemed like the right occasion."

Allie bumped the front door closed with her backside. "I feel special. Straight ahead to the kitchen."

"You are special." Not much room to get lost in the little house, but he followed her direction and set the wine and his containers on the table. Was that Dave Matthews on the stereo? It might as well have been straight from his own playlist. "Nice music."

"Thanks. Nice wine." She set her containers down and tipped the bottle to read the label. "Although way too expensive."

He hummed to himself as he opened the salad bowl. Women didn't usually complain he spent too much money on them. If anything; the opposite. "It was a gift. Was saving it for the right time, and I've been hiding it from Saralynn. Best way to do that is to get it out of the house. You're actually doing me a favor."

"Well in that case, I'll break out the big glasses." She winked and pulled two plastic goblets from a cabinet and handed him one.

The logo on the side read Humpy's in big print, and under an ugly cartoon fish, Great Alaskan Alehouse. "This is the best thing I've ever seen."

She laughed and filled each goblet halfway. "Souvenirs from grad school. I plan on getting real wine glasses soon."

"I mean it. I think these are awesome. No glasses from Boston?"

"Uh, no." She gestured for him to sit, then took the chair next to him. "When you get your master's, you think you don't have time for anything but school, but it turns out you do have time to drink. When you get your PhD, you don't leave your apartment unless you're going to the library."

He grinned and loaded some salad on his plate, then passed her the bowl and broke out the rolls. "You're pretty impressive, you know that?"

"Yep."

"And modest."

The corners of her mouth twitched as she peeled the lid back from the biggest container. "Lasagna? It smells incredible. You really did this?"

"Your doubt stings, Kally. You think Saralynn did it?"

She paused in hefting a big piece onto her place. "No. Good point. Hey, you've called her your baby sister, which leads me to think you have other siblings."

"Look how far we've come. Your freakish perception doesn't even faze me anymore." He smiled when she narrowed her eyes and nudged his elbow against hers. "Yes, I have an older sister, Shiloh, and a younger sister, Sophie. Saralynn is the baby."

"Your parents had a theme going."

He smirked. "Yeah. I was supposed to be Shannon. Imagine their surprise."

She swallowed a big forkful and took a sip of wine. "Three sisters. That explains a lot."

He stabbed a piece of lettuce and frowned. "What's that mean?"

"Wouldn't you like to know?" Mischief lit her whole face, and she swirled the wine in her glass.

"Hey." He didn't pout, but it took effort.

Allie took another sip. "I'm just messin' with ya."

But he couldn't tell if she was. "I am not above tickling you at the dinner table."

She lifted her brows. "That's a pretty serious threat. You assume you could take me."

The responding image made his jeans a little tighter. Ohh he wanted to take her. *On* the table. He directed his gaze down to his plate. They'd been flirting so long; denying the chemistry. This first date felt like the fiftieth. He didn't know how much longer he could last. Hard to tell how Allie felt. She had the super shrink thing working for her and seemed to have the will of an ox. "You keep taunting me and I may withhold dessert."

Her eyes widened, and she pulled her lower lip between her teeth. "What kind of dessert are we talking?"

Well, now he had a different kind of dessert in mind. But judging by her face, she meant confection not erection. He eyed the last unopened container. "Homemade tiramisu. Grandmom's recipe."

"I apologize for and withdraw my previous teasing."

"I thought so." He cut himself a piece of lasagna and lifted it to his dish. "Can I ask you something? Since this is our first and potentially only date? I get the feeling you know my life history since birth, so you know I've dated, had a few relationships that lasted more than a year, but nothing that hit me hard. What about you?"

She paused mid chew, and her expression ran the gamut from putting up one of her patented emotional walls to maybe showing a flicker of vulnerability. After she swallowed, she shrugged. "I had a serious boyfriend in college, and I thought it might go somewhere. Then I got injured, and things changed. If you remember, I didn't handle it well. It was world-ending at the time. I'm sure I pushed him away, but he didn't try that hard to stay."

The trace of pain in her eyes made Shane want to go a few rounds with the guy. "Idiot. Him, not you."

That got a smile from her, and she pushed around the last bite of pasta with her fork. "Thanks. Since then, I've been in grad school and establishing my career. I've dated some, but nothing that … hit me hard." Her gaze lifted to his, and her eyes said, *Until now*. At least, he hoped so.

"Crush" came on the speakers. On impulse, he stood and held out his hand. She stared at him with a mix of confusion and hesitation. He wiggled his fingers. "If it's only one date, we have to do all the date things. No family members or disapproving bosses watching."

She pursed her lips but slid her hand into his and stood. He led her to the living room and guided her free hand to his shoulder then set his on her waist and pulled her closer. Her mouth popped open in playful surprise, but she didn't pull away. He smiled down at her and swayed side to side, guiding them in small circles. There wasn't just chemistry between them. It felt more like a nuclear reaction. The proximity amplified it by ten. Her soft, sweet perfume smelled like candy, and the next thing he knew, he'd lowered his head and brushed her lips with his. Just a taste.

Allie didn't move at first, but he heard her breath catch. When it seemed like she might push him away, she tilted her head, and her lips pressed back into his. It was enough to silence any remaining doubt or reluctance. He pulled her flush against him and deepened the kiss. Her lips parted at his tongue's teasing pressure, and he couldn't help a soft moan. She tasted like sweet wine. Intoxicating.

He backed her against the wall and used both hands to pull her hips into his. If it wasn't obvious before how much he wanted her, there'd be no question now. She gasped and slid her arms around his neck, angling for more contact. Her fingers stroked the back of his neck, and it was at once sweet and hot as hell. A few more minutes of this, and there'd be no turning back. He broke the kiss and leaned his forehead against hers, panting and getting his heart rate below stroke levels. "Allie." Her name came out a ragged whisper. "Stop me before I can't stop."

She blinked, and her dark eyes focused on him. The longing there almost took out his knees. She cupped his face in her palm and slid her thumb along his cheekbone. So soft, but the impact struck deep. She licked her lips. "Part of me doesn't want you to stop. But I don't know if I'm ready to go there."

It took about thirty seconds to digest that. The first few were spent trying to get beyond the part about her wanting him to keep going. But once he did, the implication deflected the blow to his libido. "Are you saying you want another date?"

Her lips parted, and he could see the mental scramble for a denial, but the truth was out now, and there was no going back. She sighed. "God help me, but yes. I guess that's what I'm saying."

"Ha!" He picked her up for another kiss, just lifting her feet off the floor. She swatted his shoulder when he set her down.

"This doesn't change anything. We still have to be careful and professional. And I still feel guilty, but … it might be worth it. Somehow."

"I'm gonna look right past all of those qualifiers and take away from that you think we're worth it."

She grinned, and it lit him up inside like the roar of the crowd at a home game. "I thought you were working on the self deception."

"Hey, you can't take it back now. You *like* me."

"You know what'll get you more points? Tiramisu."

"Done deal."

Chapter Twenty

Monday, May 19th

Dave Matthews' "Stay" blasted from her cell phone, and Allie groaned and rolled over, slapping at it on the nightstand. "Nooo. I'm off today. The team's in Chicago." Dave persisted, and she managed to grab the phone, jam her thumb on the screen to accept the call, and hold it to her ear. "This is Dr. Kallen."

"Kally?" The voice was male and familiar but hard to place.

She squinted at the screen but didn't recognize the number. "Yes?"

"It's David. Sickavish. Mac's at Desert Springs Hospital, and I thought I should call you. She told me not to, that she's fine, but I really think she could use you here. She had some abdominal pain this morning, and they admitted her. They're running tests. You know how she likes to imagine herself Wonder Woman, but I know she's scared."

"Oh my God. I'll be there. Thanks, David." She pushed End Call and scrambled off the bed, pulling clothes out of drawers in the dark. Mac would be okay. She had to. And so would the baby.

Allie pulled her hair up in a ponytail without a brush and pushed her feet into her sneakers without breaking stride. She grabbed her keys and purse and jumped in the car. Las Vegas predawn meant the sky went from jet black to charcoal gray. The day was warming up but taking its time, and even though the city never slept, traffic was light on the way to the hospital.

She burned rubber pulling into a parking spot, jogged inside, and stopped. In her half-asleep, half-panicked state, she hadn't asked David which room they were in. Two nurses later, Allie stepped off the elevator on the third floor and found Mac and David in room three fourteen.

Mac rolled her eyes when she saw Allie, but her fear lay right under the surface. And her fingers were curled tightly around David's hand. "I told him not to call you."

"I'm glad he did."

"Before someone shoots the messenger, I think I'll get a cup of coffee. Can I get you anything, Mac?" David looked down at his wife, concern clear in his expression and tight posture.

Mac quirked a brow. "How 'bout a husband who listens?"

He bent to kiss her forehead. "Sorry. You're stuck with me. Call if you change your mind."

"I have Kally and a floor full of nurses who come running at the push of a button. I'm fine. Go." She gave his hand one more squeeze then pushed him toward the door. He paused at the threshold, but Mac gave him a look, and he kept going. She smiled at Allie and laid her head back on the pillow with a sigh. "He's sweet. But he worries too much."

"He loves you. He's allowed." She took the chair next to Mac's bed and relaxed a notch. "You're feeling okay now?"

"They gave me something for the pain, so it's hard to say. You really didn't need to come down here, Kally."

"I wanted to. I know you're fine. This is for *my* peace of mind."

Mac looked skeptical. "If you say so."

"I do."

"Hey Kally?"

"If you're going to ask about Shane, this might not be the time."

"Now that you mention it, I want to hear *all* about it. But first, I was going to inquire about your Irish ensemble."

Allie looked down at herself. Green running shorts and an orange t-shirt. Oops. Nothing said anxiety like a mismatched outfit. "You don't like it? I just wear this around the house."

"Even on your grubby hermit days you color coordinate. I tease you about your sweats, but they match. You're worried, too."

She considered denying it, but Mac wasn't too bad at analyzing either. "I just wanted to make sure you were okay. And baby Beckham in there."

Mac smiled and set a hand on her stomach. "Thanks. Hopefully the tests come back soon. In the mean time, I need a distraction, and *you* need to tell me what happened with Shane."

She might not be able to do much medically, but Allie could distract with the best of them, and Mac was right. It would help them both. "If you insist."

• • •

Dave Matthews began serenading again. Allie stretched in the uncomfortable hospital chair and heard her neck and spine crack in at least three places. After going over every detail of the date twice, she'd taken turns with David running for food and coffee. The first round of Mac's tests showed she and the baby were probably okay but weren't definitive enough for the OB, so they were trying again, and the day had stretched into night. Somehow, they'd all fallen asleep, shot nerves or not.

She dug her phone out of her purse, silenced the ringer, and checked the time. Eight o'clock, and Shane was calling. She tiptoed out of the room and eased the door closed behind her. "Hello?"

"Allie." A long, soft sigh, and relief in his voice. "We lost tonight. I lost."

"I'm sorry." And she was, even though it was hard to focus on anything but Mac. The game had to have just ended, and the first thing he did was call her. Shane, who didn't talk to *anyone* after a loss. "What happened?"

Silence for a minute. "I couldn't get in the zone. I'm used to looking over and seeing you by the glass, and when I didn't … I don't know. It just didn't feel right."

Oh boy. Superstitions were well and good when they revolved around inanimate objects. When they centered on people, things got bad. "You were the number one goaltender in the league before you even met me. The magic's in you. It's sweet that you like me there, and you know I want to cheer you on, but I can't be at every game."

"I swear you're not my lucky jockstrap. I just feel better when you're here. It's like I can focus."

Still sweet, but still dependency. Sometimes she wished she could switch off the shrink. "I can give you some mental exercises for that. I promise you are capable of winning all on your own."

He went quiet for a beat. "Okay. You're right. Besides, if it comes down to seeing you on or off ice, I choose off."

She smiled. "Me too."

"You have no idea how happy that makes me. I know you probably won't accept, but I have a ticket to Wednesday's game for you waiting at Will Call. If you're worried about feeding my superstition, you don't even have to let me know you're there until after the game. It's not about luck. I just miss you."

God. Why was this so hard? It was silly because they'd seen each other forty-eight hours ago, but she missed him, too.

"You don't have to answer now. Just think about it. How was your day?"

Concern for her best friend flooded back, and she curled her free arm around her stomach. "Ah, not so good. Mac's in the hospital. She had some abdominal pains, and they're running tests, making sure the baby's okay."

"God, I'm sorry. How is she?"

Despite everything, it felt good to have him to lean on, even over the phone. She closed her eyes and let the tension fall away. "She's okay. It looks like everything is all right. They're just making extra sure."

His voice dropped a note. "How are you?"

It had been a long time since someone other than Mac or her parents cared enough to ask that, and it filled a space she hadn't known was empty. "I'm fine. Thanks."

"I wish I could be there."

So do I. Scary thought. "You're exactly where you need to be. I'll email you the exercises, and you will kick ass on Wednesday. Maybe we can have that second date when you're back on Friday."

"That is the best thing I've heard all day. In the mean time, call me if you need anything?"

"Sure. Back atcha."

"Careful what you wish for."

Chapter Twenty-One

Wednesday, May 22nd

Allie navigated the suburbs until she found Mac's house, a cute two-story with a yard too green for Vegas. She scooped up the get-well basket then hopped out of the car and beeped it locked. Mac opened the front door in a soccer jersey and sweat pants, but to her credit, the pants were from Victoria's Secret, and she *was* color coordinated in blue and white. Allie smiled. "Hey, Mama. You look good. How are you feeling?"

Mac tucked an auburn strand behind her ear and stepped out of the way so Allie could come in. "I'm fine. Really. You know the tests came back okay. And they kept me the extra day for observation. I'm surprised I succeeded in keeping you away this long."

Allie headed for the kitchen. "You were pretty clear that I needed to go home and sleep. And change because my outfit wasn't up to standard. How's this?"

Mac trailed behind and took a seat on a stool at the breakfast bar. She did a quick scan then gave a thumbs-up. "Trouser jeans and a pinstripe blouse. Much better. You working today?"

Allie set the basket on the counter, then poured herself a cup of coffee and got a glass of ice water for her friend. "Not officially. The team's still away, so as far as management's concerned, I'm not on duty until they get back."

"But?"

"But the dance team is still here, and this is a good time to work them in while the guys are away."

"*I* don't see anything wrong with it, but I feel like this is going to bite you in the butt eventually."

Probably. But how could she turn her back on people who actually needed her? Allie sighed and sipped her coffee. "I'll deal with that when and if it happens."

"That's my ostrich girl." Mac eyed the basket. "That looks an awful lot like a present."

"Oh yeah. For you, apple-scented bubble bath, lotion, and spa mitts and slippers for a day of relaxation before you go back to work. And for baby Beckham, a plush soccer ball."

Mac almost chocked on her water. "You are the best ever. Now catch me up. Anything new with Hot Skates?"

"Ugh." Allie hung her head. "They lost Monday night. He called me after and said he focuses better when I'm there."

"Aww."

"No 'aww.' It's not good. I can't be at every game. He can't depend on me that way. I'm not a rabbit's foot. I gently pointed that out, and he agreed. They play again tonight. He put a ticket on hold for me and said to think about it, but even if I wanted to, it's too late now. We have a tentative date when he gets back on Friday."

"You should go, Kally." Mac's eyes sparked the way they used to right before she suggested something crazy like climb the water tower to watch meteors or flash the frat boys watching their soccer practice.

"What?"

"To Chicago. Go to McCarran and hop on the next flight. You don't have any set appointments today. You could just make it if you left now."

"Do I need to list the twenty ways that could blow up in my face?"

Mac tilted her head with innocent doe eyes.

"Okay, fine. One, if he sees me and he wins, he'll keep thinking I'm his personal four-leaf clover."

"Wear a hat and take a bathroom break every time the team enters or exits the ice. Next?"

"What if someone from management sees me hanging around after the game? What's my reason for being there?"

"Leave with the rest of the crowd and have Shane meet you in your hotel room."

"All right, then the most obvious. I've been on *one* date with this guy, and I'm going to fly cross-country for one night?"

"Kally." Mac set her water down and curled her hand around Allie's. "When's the last time you followed your heart instead of that big brain barely contained in your pretty head? Seriously. It's incredible it doesn't drag on the ground."

Allie stuck out her tongue.

"I mean it. This amazing man can't go two days without seeing you and begged you to come. Is it crazy? Maybe. I'm sure it doesn't fit in your logic box. But it's the most romantic thing I've ever heard of, the kind people dream about, and you deserve it. You wouldn't be doing this for Shane. Do it for you." And then she brought out the big guns. "I dare you."

"Maaac." Allie frowned.

"You may think you're too evolved for the dare to work anymore with all your psych training, but admit it. You just felt the twinge of a challenge."

Damn it, she did. But more troubling, she felt a rush of excitement and anticipation at the thought of flying out to see Shane play knowing how much he wanted her there. "Okay. But if this goes wrong, you will never hear the end of it."

"I'll take that bet."

• • •

Wednesday Night

Allie dove into the crush of people at the United Center main doors and picked up her ticket at Will Call. The short line would be surprising at any other time, but this was the Stanley Cup conference finals, and most people going already had their tickets. Wiggling her way through the masses after that was the tough part. To blend in a little better, she pulled a Blackhawks t-shirt over her button-down, cringing inside that she was supporting the enemy. But a Sinners jersey would get her noticed around here and definitely stand out in the crowd.

Her stomach rumbled from the day's traveling diet of airplane cookies and airport bagels. With the two-hour time jump, she'd just barely made it to the arena before the first puck drop. Probably better to sneak in after that anyway. Concession lines dwindled down as game time approached, and she took the opportunity to snag a hot dog, soda, and popcorn. Bad for the waistline but good for the taste buds. A fair trade, and one she was more than willing to make at the moment.

She found her section and waited by the steps until a ref's whistle stopped play on the ice. When it was safe to move, she descended until she was three rows from the glass, right behind the goaltender. Luckily, Chicago was at this end for the first period, so Shane would be at the other end of the ice. *For now.* It might be wise to skip the second period altogether. Easy enough to find her spot—the one empty space in a packed house. She excused her way through rowdy fans and settled in her seat, glancing at the scoreboard. No penalties, so the whistle must have been for icing or off sides.

The puck dropped in the Sinners defensive zone, and since that was too far away to keep track of without staying glued to the Jumbotron screen, she took a minute to look around. Chicago's crowd was just as spirited as Vegas', but not as … flashy. Vegas fans tended to have glitter face paint, light-up glow horns, and sometimes feather boas. This arena was a sea of red and black with some foam fingers thrown in as accessories.

There were no lulls in this game. The teams raced back and forth from one end to the other, evenly matched. It would come down to the goalies, and that could be good or bad. Maybe she *should* let Shane know she was there. The professional stakes were high. But so were the personal ones. The thing about lucky charms in sports was that once they stopped working, they were treated like the plague. He might be glad to have her around when he was winning, but if he lost while she was there—even though he cared for her and some part of his brain knew she wasn't a mojo-killer—he might not want to see her anymore; personally or professionally. Why did it always have to be lose-lose?

The Blackhawks got a breakaway, and Patrick Kane torpedoed toward the Sinners' zone. It would take a miracle to stop him. He leaned his weight into the shot, and with some kind of super human power, Shane put up his glove and snatched the puck out of the air without even looking. Allie jumped out of her seat and screamed, clapping until her hands hurt. The sea of fans looked at her oddly, and some with anger. The man next to her shook his head. "No, hon. He didn't make the shot. No goal."

Duh. Allie almost said as much, then looked down at her shirt and remembered she was supposed to be blending in. "Oh … I thought it went in. I mean, no way he could have missed, right?" The man shrugged, and the people around her did too. *Phew.* That was close.

The first period ended with the teams tied at one. Allie stayed in her seat while everyone else went to stretch their legs. It was a nice break to let go of the tension ball that filled her chest every time Shane had to make a save. Chicago's dance team, the Bud Light Ice Crew, did a number and shot t-shirts into the crowd. Even though they were barely clothed, they were modest compared to the Lady Sinners. She stayed to watch the Zambonis glide around, but when they finished and the lights went back up, Allie hot-footed it out of her row and up the steps to the main concourse.

Couldn't risk Shane making a play behind the net and glancing up to see her.

This time, she got a bottle of water and a box of chocolate-covered peanuts at the concession and stood at a tall table under a screen showing the action on the ice. It should be less anxiety-inducing, but she could still hear every whistle, roar and boo about twenty feet away. Both teams scored once more and remained even going into the third period. Allie stared at the stairway. She could go back and watch the end or go to her hotel and remove herself as a luck charm, either good or bad. She headed for the door.

Chapter Twenty-Two

Wednesday Night: Postgame

Allie stretched out on her stomach across her hotel bed, chin propped in her hands as she watched the postgame interviews. The Sinners' victory resulted in a lot of Chicago booing, so she knew she'd made the right choice. It was too easy to get caught up in the game and cheer at the wrong times, and after that shootout win, she wouldn't have been able to help herself.

She polished off the room service hamburger and every last fry. Nothing but healthy food for the next week on her menu. And extra gym time. Starting tomorrow. Her cell phone rang, and she nearly rolled off the bed reaching for it. Shane's name on the screen. "Hello?"

"D'you see the game?" Male chatter in the background, but he spoke loud enough, and she could hear the smile in his voice.

"I did." Why not keep him in suspense for a little longer?

"So either you made it out and laid low, or you were right and I have to make my own luck."

"Or both."

"You're here?" The excitement in his tone made her heart flip-flop.

"I left before the third period just in case you won and thought it was because of me. Now you know you did it on your own."

"You are full of surprises. How about we have our date early? I can meet you somewhere."

"I saw the end of the game on TV. After that last save you made, you're a wanted man here. There may be mobs. Also, it's probably not a good idea to be seen in public together. I'm having trouble rationalizing my presence to myself let alone the media. Or worse; Nealy."

He snickered then went quiet for a minute, probably imagining the horror of explaining to his coach that he was dating his therapist. Annnd the guilt was back. "Well, I'll come to you. Where are you staying?"

Indecision gnawed at her gut. The whole point of flying out to see him was to *see* him, but what did it imply to invite him to her hotel room?

"I promise I'm not expecting anything. You came all the way here, and I just want to hang out for a while. Unwind. I have an early flight back in the morning, so I can't stay out late anyway. You know, Coach does bed checks like a camp counselor."

Allie smiled. She'd just bet Nealy *would* do that. "I'm at the Fairfield Inn and Suites downtown, room two sixteen."

"I'll see you in twenty."

• • •

Adrenaline pumped through Shane as the taxi dropped him in front of the hotel. Crazy. He'd just faced down frozen pucks speeding at him over one hundred miles an hour, but seeing *Allie* was what got his blood going. He kept his head bowed through the lobby. Thankfully, in his suit, he looked like any other business traveler, and no one paid attention. He took the stairs to the second floor and found two sixteen. His pulse pounded in his ears as he knocked. When she opened the door, he grinned, then took in her shirt. "Traitor."

Her eyes widened in surprise and confusion until she followed his gaze. She lifted a shoulder. "I keep forgetting about this thing. I bought it to blend in so the Chicago crowd wouldn't flog me or torture me on the big screen. And I didn't want you to be able to spot me."

He scoffed playfully and stepped inside, closing the door behind him. "You can take it off now."

That blush filled her whole face, and God, was it cute.

"The t-shirt. I just meant the t-shirt."

"Right." She ducked into the bathroom, closing the door.

He took a seat on one of the queen beds, trying to regain control, but images of her stripping down weren't easy to banish. It was just the two of them here in a hotel room. He *had* just wanted to hang out, talk about the game and hell, *be* with her. Not in the carnal sense; not originally, but now …

The bathroom door opened, and Allie emerged in her work clothes sans traitor shirt. She'd also undone her braid, and her dark hair fell in loose waves a few inches past her shoulders. Tousled. Sexy. She sat on the bed opposite him, hands on knees, and it was a struggle not to look at the subtle showing of cleavage.

He swallowed and met her gaze. "So you proved you can be at the game or not, and I can still pull out a win."

"Actually, *you* proved that, but same results."

"Mmmhmm. Pretty smart. Not that I'm surprised."

She did an *oh golly* shrug. "As long as we're giving out compliments, that save you made on Kane was the best I've ever seen. Seriously. I almost got busted because I cheered."

"That's my girl." The words came naturally and without thought. It felt right even though he had no right to claim that yet. Time to change that. Her expression softened, and her lips parted, but he cut her off. "I'm in this, Allie. I don't need a second date to tell me. I know. I knew that night at the soccer complex. This thing between us, it's different. It's big. And I want to give it a chance. Do you?"

Well, score one for him. For the first time, she didn't seem to know what to say. So why did the victory feel so terrifying? He saw tenderness and reservation in her face. God, she was going to turn him down. He stood, ready to leave, when her hand squeezed his and held him still.

"I'm here, aren't I?" She'd leaned over to reach him and exposed more of the soft curves of her breasts. On purpose?

"Is that a yes?" The words came out low and barely more than a whisper.

She stood, hesitated, then stepped into him, curling a hand around the back of his neck to pull him down for a kiss. Her lips brushed his tentatively at first and then again with more heat and conviction.

His whole body ignited. He slid both arms around her waist and pulled her closer as he kissed her back. Every kiss was like the first—wildly exciting, intense, and raw. She arched her back, pressing her chest even more firmly against his, and he pulled back with a shuddering breath. Staring at her through hooded eyes, he met her gaze. "I didn't come here for this."

"I know."

"If you're not sure—"

She stared into his eyes—into his soul—and proved her certainty. "I've never been a risk-taker. But I never met a risk worth taking before. I know there'll be consequences. And I am scared. But I want this, too."

He grinned and cupped her face in his hands, capturing her mouth in another kiss, this one soft, deep, and slow burning. The small coos of encouragement from her almost took the last of his restraint. She slid the suit jacket off his shoulders, and he let it fall. While her fingers went to work on the buttons of his shirt, he repaid the favor with hers. Pants were next. When they were down to underwear, he took a step back and drank her in.

Matching white satin bra and panties contrasted with her lightly browned skin. Tan lines showed her general preference for sports bras and racerback tanks. He closed the distance again, pulling her close and leaning her back on the bed.

• • •

Allie's heart raced like a jackrabbit, but it was just as much from excitement as it was nerves. This might be a colossally bad idea, but she'd never wanted someone more in her life. It had been so long. And dear Lord, the man looked twice as good out of his clothes as in them.

He rested heavily between her legs, and with only panties and briefs between them, not a lot was left to the imagination. At the same time, there were too many damn clothes. Shane trailed hungry kisses from the base of her neck up behind her ear, hitting a sweet spot, and she bowed against him. Mistake, because she felt him smile before he focused on that specific area, flicking it with his tongue then sucking gently.

She slid her hands along his back, trying to press him closer even though that was physically impossible. As if sensing her urgency, he unhooked her bra and tossed it aside, then rid them of their final clothing. He kneeled before her, almost reverent. "You are … perfect."

Her cheeks burned, and she smiled. She'd never been self-conscious before, but she felt naked on more than one level. Like he could see her soul as well as her body, and liked the view. "You're not so bad yourself." Massive understatement. Shane would have been an exact replica of the David if Michelangelo had used more marble in a certain area. A lot more.

The need in his eyes made her stomach flutter. He leaned over the side of the bed, giving her another amazing view, and she had a new appreciation for all the squats he did on off days. Clothing rustled on the floor, and he returned with a gold foil packet. He rested a hand on her knee, and his expression softened. "Allie, are you really—"

She sat up, cupped his cheek and cut him off with a tender kiss. "Yes. I want this. I want you." Honesty felt terrifying but freeing, like jumping out of a plane and trusting your chute to catch you. She was tired of pretending she didn't feel what she did. Tired of lying to him and to herself.

He kissed her again, and the pure sweetness of it made her heart ache. This wasn't just sex for him either. Shane slid the condom on and eased her down again, one hand cradling her shoulder blade and the other on the small of her back. His job demanded a certain toughness, but he was so careful with her.

He entered her slowly, his gaze locked on hers. The intimacy touched her in usually guarded places, and she let him in—body and heart. It took a while to adjust to the size of him, but he seemed happy to take his time. When he slid all the way home, he buried his face in her neck and sighed her name on an exhale. She held him tightly and gasped, nearly going over the edge right there.

After a long, amazing minute of simply absorbing the way he filled her, his hips started a gentle rhythm while he kissed whatever skin his lips touched. Electric. Had it ever felt like this before? Her hands wandered over his body. Smooth, soft skin covering rock hard muscle. His mouth claimed hers again, taking and giving in equal measure as he claimed her in every way that mattered.

He increased the tempo, and she held onto his hips, so close to losing it. He was too, judging by the hitch in his breath and the low moans that drove her crazy. "Shane ... yes ... please." The whispered words escaped without thought, but she couldn't regret them. She was so close. So close.

It was all the encouragement he needed. He thrust faster, harder, until he slid deep, stiffened, and she felt him pulse inside. She followed right after, arching beneath him and crying out. Broken, beautiful sounds rumbled in his throat as they rode out the aftershocks together. He collapsed, resting most of his weight on her. Still reeling, she stroked the back of his neck. He trembled under her touch. His heart beat so hard she felt it trying to out-pace her own.

For a long moment, they laid still. She didn't want to move. Ever. At least not until morning. He leaned up on his forearms; an impressive feat because she couldn't even wiggle her toes. His lips grazed hers, and he stared at her with what looked admiration, awe, and something else she was too afraid to name.

"That was incredible. Can we repeat it please?"

"Right now?"

"Ah, no. I'm only a man, Kally."

Silly to be embarrassed after what they'd just done, but there seemed to be no limits on his ability to surprise her. "Well good. Because I'm down for the count tonight. But yes, a repeat in the future would be good."

"Glad we're on the same page." He kissed her again, languid but sensual. His gently probing tongue made her reconsider the possibility of another round, but he withdrew carefully, pulling a gasp from them both. He got up to dispose of the condom. When he returned, he sat on the edge of the mattress and stared down at her.

"What?" She sat up against the headboard, pulling the sheet up over her chest.

"Is there anything you're *not* good at?"

She rolled her eyes and swatted his bicep.

He caught her hand and kissed her knuckles. "I mean it. You're scary smart. Funny. Gorgeous. And I don't mean to be a pig, but that was—"

"Gold medal sex."

"*Yes*. I'm glad it wasn't just me. One more area we're seriously compatible." He still held her hand and slid his thumb over the back of it "We're screwed, aren't we?"

Her heart ached at the real-world mental intrusion. She pursed her lips and nodded, not trusting her voice. There were only two ways for them to be together—either he quit his job, or she lost hers. He'd never quit; not that she'd let him. And she'd worked her whole life for the job she had now. It was more than a career. It was a chance to help people and change their lives in a big way. There was no way she could have predicted how Shane would change hers.

He kissed her forehead for a long minute then stood. "I wish I could stay."

"Go. Or you'll suffer the wrath of Nealy. Plus the team might fine you if you miss your flight tomorrow morning."

"Only one thing could make me leave this room right now, and it's not the fine."

Allie laughed. No one wanted to see the pixie coach angry. "Understood."

He got dressed and paused by the edge of the bed. "For the record, even though we're not sure how we're going to work this out, we're still giving it a chance." A statement—but clearly seeking validation.

All of her reservations rose to the surface. If she really were as smart as he said, she'd end it now and save them both the jobs they loved. But she couldn't deny what she felt, what she'd experienced. It was too strong. And the way he looked at her now sealed the deal. He was *afraid* she'd push him away. It was clear in his gaze. He'd shed his emotional armor. For her. She nodded.

The straight line of his shoulders relaxed, and that easy smile came back. "I'll see you on Friday. Goodnight, Allie."

"Goodnight, Shane." She watched him go, then leaned her head back and slid down onto the pillows. "I must be a world-class masochist."

Chapter Twenty-Three

Friday, May 24th

Incessant knocking. Shane grumbled and pulled his pillow over his head. That muted the sound but didn't alleviate it entirely. He growled and checked the time on his phone. Six thirty. A good half hour before he needed to be awake for the morning skate. Before he got out of bed, he squeezed his eyes shut, sucked in a deep breath, and exhaled the urge to strangle his sister. He padded across the thick carpet, eyes still half-closed, and cracked open his door. "What?"

"Good morning to you, too, grumpy bear. I just wanted to make sure you had your tux dry-cleaned."

"My what?" He didn't need a tux for his date with Allie. Wait, how did Saralynn know about that anyway?

"Your tux. The shiny black suit with the bow tie."

"I don't need my tux for—"

"*I'm* organizing this event, and the tux is required." Hand on hip, ponytail swinging with her head-tilt. The most serious he'd ever seen her.

Event. His date was not an "event." And Saralynn was most definitely not planning it. "I appreciate your interest and concern in my life, but I've got it handled."

"This isn't about your life. Not everything's about you."

Could she possibly get the irony of those words coming from her mouth? He tried to formulate a coherent response, but she beat him to it, drumming her nails on her hip.

"This is *my* thing. My time to shine. The least you can do is wear what I picked out."

"Sare, you're not Ma. And even Ma didn't dress me for my dates."

"Date? Skates and Plates is tonight. The whole team dresses up and serves generous patrons dinner at the arena. Sound familiar? I planned it this year. You know that."

Oops. He *knew* that. And it had completely skipped his mind somewhere in the space of a week. Between games and Allie, he'd lost track.

"Oh God. You forgot." The horror on her face was almost funny. He bit the inside of his cheek to keep from laughing as she pushed past him and went for his closet. She rifled through hangers until she came to one with a plastic bag and checked inside. A huge sigh deflated her angry posture. "We're lucky you're anal and had it cleaned after the last event. Now remember. You have to be lined up in the lobby with the rest of the team at six sharp."

Who was this organized alien who had taken over his sister's body? Maybe the internship really was a good thing. He'd never seen her so focused or care about something so much. Other than herself. "Six sharp. Got it."

She grinned so big, she looked twelve again and jumped into his arms. "Thanks, big brother. I really love this job."

His heart melted, and he kissed the side of her head. "I really love you."

"Aww." She leaned back and lightly slugged his arm. "Don't tell Shiloh and Sophie, but you're my favorite."

"Back atcha."

Saralynn beamed and bounced out of the room, leaving him with a disappointing realization. A team fundraiser meant no date.

• • •

"So was it …?" Mac wiggled her eyebrows.

Allie folded her arms on the table and buried her face in them. "Yes. It was perfect."

144

"Really? 'Cause that's not the universal sign for happy. And people are watching."

She sat up nonchalantly and looked around. The curious diners at Earl of Sandwich turned away, returning to their meals. Allie directed her attention to her berry, chicken, and almond salad. Even though no one was likely to hear them over the general din, she lowered her voice. "I'm too happy. That's the problem."

Mac stared at her with lowered brows and a flat mouth, as if she were solving a puzzle. "I've seen you happy, Kally, and this ain't it."

"I really like him, Mac. I …" *Love him.* Whoa. Way too soon for that. And yet, all the signs were there. "After Wednesday night, I'll never be able to get professional distance back. Not with him."

"Be honest. Professional distance walked out the door when he walked in. He's not just some patient. He's the best guy you've ever met. And I know. I've met the others."

Allie pushed her salad around with her fork. Mac wasn't lying.

"You are your own proof. After your injury, you were the most focused, determined person I'd ever seen. You wouldn't let anything stand between you and this career path. The fact you're even considering doing something that might change your course has to tell you how much it means to you. How much *he* means to you."

"Okay, okay." She stabbed a piece of chicken and chewed out her frustration. "You're right. I'm not saying this will end in happily ever after. Chances are it won't. But before you bring out the 'd' word again, I'll save you the trouble. I'll consider this with an open mind. Promise."

Mac squinted. "Then what's with the lemon face?"

"I still feel like one of those creepy high school teachers getting involved with a student."

"One, you're the same age as this man. He is definitely, and I mean *definitely*, not a little boy. Two, since he is a fully grown, big, beautiful—"

"*Mac.*"

"Sorry. Sidetracked. Since he is an adult, he's perfectly capable of making his own, informed choices, and he's chosen you, babe. So stop with the why-me's and embrace the yip-ees!" She danced in her seat to emphasize the last word.

Allie laughed and kept her head down as she forked a berry. "I don't know you."

"You mean you love me."

"Yes. That's what I meant." Dave Matthews crooned from her purse. She checked the readout on her phone. Shane. "Speak of the Sinner." She cradled it to her ear and pushed Talk. "Hey, what's up?"

"Saralynn woke me up at six thirty to remind me about Skates and Plates tonight. I'm gonna have to rain check our date. But if we win tomorrow night, I'll have a free week before finals start."

She chewed her lip. Could it be a sign? The team function wasn't his fault, but maybe it was fate stepping in.

"Please don't take this opportunity to kick me to the curb. You're all I can think about. If I could clone myself in six hours, I'd do it just so I could keep our date."

Allie smiled and shook her head. "We'll make another one."

His sigh sounded relieved. "You won't regret this."

Probability was not on her side there, but no reason to bring that up now. "I'm at lunch with Mac. Talk to you later, okay?"

"Absolutely. Say hi for me. And Allie? I'm really sorry about tonight. I was looking forward to it."

"Me too. We'll figure it out. Bye, Shane." She ended the call and dropped the phone back in her purse. Mac's gaze was burning holes in her before she even looked up. "He says hi."

"And?"

"He forgot about Skates and Plates tonight. I remember seeing flyers for it around the arena, but I forgot, too. So we have to rain check."

Mac pointed a finger at her. "That is not a sign from fate."

"I didn't say that."

"But you were thinking it."

Allie stuck her tongue out. She needed to get friends who didn't know her so well.

• • •

Ten minutes to five, and there had been a steady flow of players and dancers all day. Cole for his leadership concerns, Scotty for his lingering superstitions, and Miranda with an ex-boyfriend update. Baby the Chihuahua was back at home. Allie yawned into her hand and stood.

Two sharp knocks, then her door swung open, and Nealy appeared in an emerald skirt suit, which was different. The no-nonsense look was the same. "Hey, Doc. Can you come to the game tomorrow night? I think it would help some of the guys."

Guys? Plural? That's all she needed. More dependents. "Help?"

"You know how athletes are. Somethin' gets in their heads, good luck getting it out. They seem to have taken a shine to you and always come back to the locker room sans bullshit after a session. Whatever you're doing, it's working, and we could use some of that to take the Western Conference tomorrow. I don't want this one to go past five games."

Allie must have topped Nealy by half a foot at least, but she still felt small in the coach's presence. She tried not to cower. "I—I'm not sure that's a good idea. I don't want them to see me as Sinbad, the mascot. If they started to rely on me being there—"

"Hon, you're a good doctor, and you've gotten through to these guys, which isn't easy. I would know. But if their play depended on one person in the audience instead of their hard work, they'd have to answer to me, and they know it. I just think it'd do something for morale if they knew you were there supporting them. Like it or not, they've adopted you."

Nealy made it sound like she was delivering terminal news, but the words warmed Allie from the inside out. All the empty office hours and walking on eggshells trying not to spook players away. It worked. They liked her. "Well, how can I say no to that?"

"That's what I like to hear. Come a little early so they can see you before they leave the locker room. Jacey always gives a speech, but you just have to be there."

"Then I will be there."

Nealy nodded once. "Now, I need to report for Skates and Plates. I'm serving too."

Allie sucked her teeth trying not to laugh. She could picture diners afraid to look up from their menus, and Lord help them if an order came out wrong. "I'll see you at the game."

Nealy saluted and left. Allie stretched and sighed. Tomorrow would be interesting.

Chapter Twenty-Four

Saturday, May 25th

At five thirty, Allie key-fobbed into the basement entrance. Since she wasn't officially working, she wore jeans, ankle boots, and a long-sleeved Sinners t-shirt with the logo in rhinestones. They winked and glittered under the overhead fluorescents, a mini Las Vegas light show on her chest. Loud, echoing voices made her look up. Most of the team stood in a circle outside the locker room in the open space at the end of the hallway. The physical therapy door, usually open, was closed, and in a second she saw why.

The guys kicked around a soccer ball like it was a hacky sack, using their ankles, thighs, chests, anything but their hands. They laughed and jibed, completely oblivious to her presence until Scotty kicked the ball high and out of bounds directly at her. A spike of excitement jolted through her, and she skipped forward a step to head butt the ball straight up. When it came down, she balanced it on her knee for a few seconds then popped it onto the toe of her boot before kicking it back to them, a high lob that sent it into the middle of the circle.

Shocked cackles echoed off the concrete walls, and Dylan Cole waved her over. "C'mere, Kally. You belong here more than any of us."

Kevin Scott snorted. "Speak for yourself, Cole. This is *my* game. I just hit it from a bad angle."

"Whatever, Scotty." Cole edge over so Allie could squeeze in.

Pleasant surprise marked Shane's face from across the circle, and his smile nearly caused her to take a ball to the nose. At the last second, she butted it to him, and he chest-bumped it to Ben Collier.

Allie stole quick glances at Shane while keeping track of the ball. In black mesh shorts and an un-tucked white t-shirt, he looked relaxed, happy, in his element. He blended right in. She hit the ball with the inside of her elbow when it came her way. "You guys do this before every game?"

"Every game." Scotty caught the ball on one ankle, tossed it up, then caught it on the other ankle in a little jig.

"Quit showin' off, douche," from Collier.

"Yo, lady present." Shane sent her a silent apology.

"Huh? Oh. Sorry, Kally."

She laughed. "No sweat." Not like she wasn't used to it. "I guess I usually get here too late to see this."

"Why are you here? Not that we don't want you. I'll shut up now." Cole ducked his head. Man, she was just embarrassing everybody tonight.

"Nealy invited me." Not *Coach* because that would sound official and irk them. "I came early 'cause this could be the conference clincher, and I figured traffic would be crazy. Is that okay?"

Enthusiastic yeahs all around. Shane gave her a quick wink and, made her heart back flip. None of the other guys seemed to notice. The locker room doors swung open, and Nealy poked her head out. "Okay, time. Get in here and down to business. Warm up is in fifteen."

The team filed inside, but Shane hung back. When the doors closed behind the last of his teammates, he took two quick strides, pressed her against the wall and kissed her deeply.

Shock and raw heat kept her from reacting at first, but reason returned a beat later, and she pushed him back by the shoulders. "Are you out of your mind?" she whispered.

"I'm just happy to see you," he whispered back.

"Well don't get too happy. You have to go in there in a second, and those shorts don't hide much."

He glanced down and grinned, then pushed into the locker room. Her heart pounded. She felt her forehead. Her temperature must have jumped five degrees. Now was not the time to reenact their rendezvous, but after that kiss, it was hard to think about anything else.

With a little time to kill, she holed up in her office and laid on the couch. No one would have thought anything of her hanging out in the locker room. Athletes let go of modesty pretty fast, and men were better about it than women. But *she* wasn't comfortable seeing the whole team in their skivvies or less. She still had to be able to keep a straight face when Scotty came by talking about lucky jockstraps. Sharp clicking caught her attention, and she hopped up, peeking out her door.

Jacey strode toward the locker room in her usual game suit and killer heels. She pivoted at the sound of company and smiled. "Hey, Allie. How's it going? I hear you're a hot ticket with the team now."

A small burst of fear bloomed in her chest, but she kept it off her face. "Hot ticket?"

"Yeah, Nealy tells me they've really taken a liking to you and actually make appointments of their own free will."

The surge of relief made her lightheaded. "Yeah, I guess I'm not cursed anymore."

"You're here for the game, right? Come on with me."

Allie locked her office and trailed Jacey; second and third thoughts about dating a player tumbling through her brain. The guys, fully dressed, looked up from the benches when they walked in. Allie leaned against the wall, but Jacey stood in the middle of the room and wished them luck. The guys responded with a positive roar. Shane's dimples flashed, and those second and third thoughts got locked in the penalty box.

The team lumbered toward the ice, followed by Nealy and Jacey. Allie tagged behind and stood by the glass. The arena was *alive* with energy, and not a single seat was empty. You could feel it humming off the ice and in the crowd. This game could send the Sinners to the Cup finals, and everyone in the building knew it. Of course Nealy wanted her here tonight. Even a perceived edge could make the difference. *All right. I'm a rabbit's foot.*

The action was non-stop from the first puck drop. The Blackhawks clearly knew their back was against the wall because they played hard and dirty when they had to, garnering their share of penalties. The Sinners tried to capitalize on all the power plays, but the teams were tied at zero at the end of the first period. She held her breath to avoid the stench when the guys clomped past on their way to the locker room, and she ducked out of the way to avoid the fans dangling over the railings, in an attempt to touch their favorite players.

Cole was first off the ice and held his glove up for a fist bump. She obliged, but before she could lower her hand, the rest of them followed suit. Bump. Bump. Bump. Shane was the last in line, and when he bumped, he caught her eye and flashed those pearly whites that had the teenage girls swooning over her shoulder.

"Reese! Reese!"

He beamed at them and lifted his glove so they could touch it. They squealed and giggled, their night made. Allie used every last bit of restraint not to roll her eyes. Not that she was jealous. It would just be nice for Shane's ego to still fit in one room at the end of the season. Nealy brought up the rear of her team and patted Allie's shoulder as she went by. The tiny woman might have looked calm to a casual observer, but the straight set of her shoulders said the guys were in for an ear-chewing. It didn't matter that the Blackhawks hadn't gotten a point either. If they weren't scoring, they weren't winning. Thank God Nealy didn't want her in the room to witness the reaming.

The second period didn't slow down any, and both teams fought hard. Literally. It was a miracle the officials didn't need a calculator to keep track of all the penalty minutes. When the Sinners finally scored, the celebratory roar from the crowd was like being hit by a sonic blast. Allie cheered along with them, jumping and screaming and slapping the glass. The guys looked over, grinned and pointed at her, but she wasn't going to be embarrassed by her enthusiasm. At least, not until she looked up and saw a replay of her spaz attack on the Jumbotron screen. In high definition, she looked soup-cans-in-the-baby-carriage crazy, and she just barely kept from sprinting to hide in the ladies' room. The arena echoed with laughter, but not in a mean way. Eh, she was hardly the strangest fan there. And besides, a little public humiliation every now and then was good for the soul.

The buzzer sounded, and the guys filed off again, lifting their gloves for fist bumps. This time, they added "Yeah Kally!" to the ritual. Shane said, "Yeah Allie!" but she was the only one who caught the difference. Even Nealy gave her a big grin on the way to the locker room. Hard to define the duties of a rabbit's foot, but she must be doing it right. Even though her reservations about coming had been well-founded, it was good to be part of a team again.

The Lady Sinners and Sinbad skipped onto the ice, and the announcer's voice boomed. "Alllll right! It's time for 'Show me a sign!' Hold your signs up while we scan the crowd. The best sign wins season tickets for next year! Ready? Shooooow me a sign!"

Allie watched the contest on the big screen. There were simple, cutesy signs like *Sinners are winners!* But the most entertaining were the ones propositioning players. *I want Scotty's body! I want to roll with Cole! Collier, marry me, eh? I want a piece of Reese!* Okay, that one wasn't so funny. An irrational part of her brain wanted a piece of the woman holding that sign. Jeez. What was happening?

The camera landed on one fan, lights flashed, and bells and whistles sounded. "We have a winner!" The sign said: *What stays in Vegas? The CUP!* The whole arena cheered in clear agreement, and the sign-holder almost took a flying leap several rows down in his manic excitement. The Cup better stay in Vegas. Or her appointment book would be even more full.

When the third period started, the Sinners could not be stopped. Whatever Nealy had said to them lit a fire. They weaved and dodged with unearthly grace and speed, owning the puck the whole time. The Blackhawks might have touched it twice, including their goalie, who let three more get past him to the crowd's irrepressible elation.

The final buzzer sounded, and the Sinners' bench emptied onto the ice. The guys embraced, laughing and jumping into one big pile. Shane did a belly flop on top. Allie couldn't stop smiling. After a few minutes of celebration, the men climbed to their feet and lined up for handshakes. The Blackhawks looked solemn for the most part, but some congratulated certain Sinners they probably knew from playing together on other teams.

That was one thing she'd never had to experience—changing teams. It had to be hard leaving friends and getting used to playing against them. No wonder the rumors had hit Shane so hard—the idea of getting traded *now* when he'd have to go it alone. But if his performance tonight were any indicator, he'd be in Vegas as long as he wanted. The thought of him moving made her heart ache, but not just in sympathy. It would hurt if he left. A lot.

The announcer's voice interrupted her thoughts. "Youuuur Sinners, Western Conference champions!" The crowd response was deafening, but it made her smile again. She clamped her hands over her ears and watched as the three stars of the game were named. Shane was number one. He glided around, lifting his stick to wild applause. When he skated off ice, he paused in front of her, pure happiness in human form. He leaned in, kissed her cheek, and winked in a promise of more before heading for the locker room. For her, the world stopped, but there were no indicators it had for anyone else except the girls gasping above her head in jealousy. What did he just do?

Chapter Twenty-Five

Monday, May 27th

Shane squinted through the sweat that dripped in his eyes and burned like a mother. He'd have to take his mask and gloves off to wipe it away, and that wasn't really an option at the moment. Hour two of working on his backside push with the goalie coach, and his ankle was a little sore, but he'd be damned before he admitted it. Nothing short of a compound fracture would take him out of the game now. The Cup was in sight. Not only that, there was no way he'd risk having to see Allie professionally again. If he had to, she'd end things for good, and he couldn't let that happen. A little soreness wasn't anything. Besides, how much longer could practice go on?

Even Dictator Nealy saw fit to give the team Sunday off after the conference final win, and she'd deemed morning skates optional until Thursday. But they were only optional if you didn't know Coach. Miss too many, and your ice time decreased, mandatory practices were harder, and you might not be a Sinner for much longer depending on your contract and her whim. But who could argue with success? No one could argue with Nealy; that was for sure.

"All right, Reese, call it a day." The goalie coach patted his shoulder and headed out.

Shane leaned against the post and shed some of his gear. He wiped his face with the towel on top of the netting, then drank what was left in his water bottle. He was the last on the ice. The air smelled like sweat and snow; like hockey. The arena was so *quiet*, but the roar of Saturday's crowd still echoed in his head. He replayed the Sinners' last goal and the pile-on after the final buzzer. But clearer than anything else, he saw Allie jumping on the sidelines, cheering. For him.

A throat cleared. He pivoted and grinned. "The psychic connection finally works both ways. I was just thinking about you."

She folded her arms across her chest. "Nealy caught me in the hall, wanted me to check on you. Said you wouldn't get off the ice."

He glided over, helmet, stick, and gloves tucked under his arms. "When Nealy says we can call it a day, she doesn't mean it. Being the last one off, I just earned some bonus points."

"She gonna give you a cookie and a gold star?"

"She'll start me on Saturday, so for her it's the same thing."

Allie's expression was hard to read. Thoughtful but reserved. That never meant anything good.

"You're worried about the other night."

She scoffed then wiped her face blank and lowered her voice. "You kissed me after the game. On television."

"I kissed your cheek. I kissed Scotty's too in the locker room. We were celebrating. No one will think anything about it. Has anyone said anything to you?"

"No … but I'm serious. We have to be really careful. You know what could happen."

"You know that poster on your office door? Follow your internal compass? Mine's pointing at you. And I think you feel the same way. At least, I hope you do." His heart beat as hard as it had during practice, his mouth felt dry, his hands cold and clammy. If he didn't officially have her, why did it feel like he had so much to lose? "Now, you owe me a date. And you strike me as the kind of person who keeps her word or dies trying. It's one of the things I like most about you."

At first, she didn't react. Then she pursed her lips to the side and narrowed her eyes in that playful way she did when she knew he had her cornered. "Well played. I'm still not convinced this is a good idea."

"It's a terrible idea. But giving up would be worse."

A wavering smile took hold on her full, beautiful lips, and her gaze held his steady and sweet. "So what do we do?"

Relief poured through his veins, and his already taxed legs almost went out from under him. He leaned a shoulder into the Plexiglas and bent his head so they were almost nose to nose. "Right now I want to kiss you more than I want to breathe."

She froze for a second, her eyes half-closed. All he had to do was tilt his head, but not without her permission. The haze seemed to clear because she stepped back, looked around, and whispered, "Well not *here*."

"Not here. That means I can kiss you somewhere else?"

He watched her try to mentally backpedal and come up against a wall. She sighed, and the corner of her mouth quirked up. "All right, yes. But you will shower first." Her nose wrinkled, and he laughed.

"That bad, huh? You don't notice it after a while."

"Maybe *you* don't."

"Okay, okay. I will shower first, and then …?"

She set her hands on her hips, distracting him. "Then you can come over my place tonight, and I will kick your butt in Just Dance."

He looked up. "You have an Xbox? Marry me."

She did an about-face, and headed for the locker room. "If that's the best you got, you're in trouble."

She had no idea.

Chapter Twenty-Six

Monday Night

The doorbell rang at six o'clock, and Allie checked her makeup one more time. *He's just a guy.* Except he wasn't, and every day that became more and more obvious. Between appointments, she found herself wondering what he was doing; if he were thinking about her. If she replayed that night in Chicago one more time, she'd combust. This couldn't possibly work. So why was she willing to risk so much for it?

The doorbell rang again, and she hopped down the short staircase to open the front door. Shane held a large, flat box from Grimaldi's Pizzeria. He grinned, and she felt warm and light inside. *Danger, Will Robinson.*

"Delivery."

"What do I owe you?"

"At least one kiss. But I do accept tips."

She turned liquid inside imagining the possibilities. "How about I let you win the warm-up round in Just Dance?"

"*Let* me, huh?" His voice dipped low and seductive, and for a second, she just stared. He wiggled the box. Oh. Right. She moved aside so he could come in then closed the door behind him and followed him to the kitchen. He set the pizza on the table and piled three slices on one of the paper plates she'd set out. "We eating here, or …?"

"TV trays in the living room. Beer in the fridge. I figure we can catch some of the Flyers-Caps game before we throw down."

His brows arched suggestively as he did a full body scan like he was imagining throwing her down on the couch and forgetting about everything else.

"Dance. Before we dance."

"Mmm." He clicked his tongue, then grabbed a beer and headed for the living room.

Allie fanned herself behind his back, picked two pieces of pizza for herself as well as a light beer, and joined him in front of the TV, where the game was already on.

Shane swallowed a giant mouthful of pepperoni and wiped the side of his mouth with the back of his hand. "Pizza, beer, hockey, and video games. You realize you're the perfect woman. How is it possible you're not already taken?"

"You mean am I secretly a Satanist or something?"

"No." He almost choked on another bite of pizza. He took a sip of beer and licked his lips. "I mean I know about College Guy, and you mentioned dating a few duds since. But you could have any man you wanted. How did I get so lucky?"

"Nice save."

He lifted a shoulder. "Kinda my specialty."

"I don't know. I put school and work first because that's what I wanted most. I wanted to help people. But maybe it was easier to focus on others' vulnerabilities than to face my own."

"What changed?" He glanced at her then shifted his gaze to the TV as he ate his second piece. He might seem distracted, but she knew better. He saw her like a scared rabbit and was giving her space to open up, whether he realized it or not. Good instincts. A common goalie trait.

She smiled to herself, but hesitated. Saying it out loud to another person would destroy her ability to bury it. But wasn't she supposed to be facing her vulnerabilities? "I still want to help people. Maybe now more than ever. My job before this was an internship with the Providence Bruins. My first patient had a severe concussion. The medical doctors kept a close eye on him and watched the physical symptoms, but he had trouble accepting the slow recovery."

"Sounds familiar."

Her mouth twitched in an almost-smile but didn't quite make it. "Well, Caleb was different. He lied to his doctors, and to me. We thought he was improving, but he only pretended. I should have seen it. I should have known."

Shane set his pizza down and angled toward her. "I think I see where this is going."

"I returned him to play. His first game back, he took a hit. It ended his career. And changed his day-to-day life. It was bad. He had to re-learn how to do simple things and couldn't be alone for months."

"That wasn't your fault. The other docs cleared him too."

She looked at her hands folded on her lap. *But I should have seen it.*

"Allie." He lifted her chin and met her gaze. "The kid lied. I'm not saying I can't understand the impulse—we both know better—but it's his own fault he went back too early. Not yours. You're a great doctor."

"You're a little biased."

"I mean it." His hand dropped from her chin to squeeze her fingers. "I never would have gotten through my block without you. And you got the whole team to come and talk to you. Without threats or bribes. I know those guys, and that's a big deal."

Warmth filled her chest and eased the aching guilt and anxiety around her heart. "Thank you."

He leaned in and kissed her, just a soft brush of his lips, but he held it for a few seconds before nudging her nose with his. It was sensual but tender, and whatever remaining emotional walls she had came crumbling down. He genuinely cared for her. It wasn't transference, and he didn't see her as one of the many. Maybe she'd known for a while and didn't want to admit it, but there was no denying it anymore. She cupped his face in one hand and slid her thumb along his cheekbone. The words were there, she just couldn't say them.

It didn't matter because understanding dawned in his eyes. He kissed her again, this time with unchecked passion. He pulled her closer, devouring until they both had to come up for air. Through hooded eyes, he stared at her, trying to catch his breath. "Allie." All at once, it sounded like a declaration, a question, and a promise.

She nodded in agreement. Her psychology background made it hard to believe in something like destiny or fate. People made their own choices, and those choices shaped their lives. But sometimes a domino chain of events looked too perfect in hindsight to write off as coincidence. If she hadn't gotten injured, she wouldn't have become a counselor, wouldn't have gotten this job or met this man. The man staring at her like she was a winning lottery ticket. The problem with dominos was they only made sense when looking back. So what now?

It was too big a question, and she didn't have the answer. Not tonight. She poked his chest. "Don't try to distract me before I claim my title as best dancer."

He studied her face a few seconds past comfortable like he was trying to connect her dots. "You're pretty confident. Then again, I've seen you dance. Maybe I should get a handicap, like we tie your hands behind your back." His eyes lit up as if the mental image inspired other uses for that, too.

She laughed, and the tension faded away. "You wish. Hey, looks like the Flyers are about to take the Eastern Conference."

They watched Philadelphia dominate St. Louis on screen with ten minutes left in the third period. There were miracles, but there was no coming back from a six-goal deficit in that little amount of time. Shane sighed. "You're right."

"You were hoping to face the Blues?"

"Between them and Philly? Hell yeah. The Flyers play gritty. Lots of fights. Players get hurt. Especially this close to the Cup.

And I don't know if you've ever been in Philadelphia for a game, but it's ... rough. The fans are as intimidating as the players."

"Sounds like good television."

"You sound like Saralynn. This morning she gave me a ten-minute speech about how a good showdown could get us more fans on the East Coast." He shook his head and sipped his beer.

"And yet you seem amused."

He snorted. "A month ago, she barely knew the name of *my* team. Now she knows every team in the league, the breakdown of divisions, and the PR opportunities of facing each one."

"The internship's been a positive thing for her."

"It's been a great thing. Don't get me wrong, I'm happy for her. I'd be happier if I didn't live with her."

Allie got up to put the video game in. "I think that's fair. You haven't lived with her in several years. Then there's the age difference."

"Hey. I'm not old."

"I didn't say you were old. Just older than her. There's a big difference between twenty-one and thirty."

"You're not making it sound any better."

She grinned as she finalized the setup and waved him to stand beside her in front of the screen. The first song came on, and they jumped into action. Well, she jumped. He spazzed. She bit the inside of her lip hard enough to draw blood. If she full out laughed at him, he might quit early.

"Not fair. This is your game. You've had practice."

"Sounds like an excuse to me. I wonder what Nealy would say about that?"

His jaw dropped open and he scoffed, making his movements sharper. "Okay, it's on."

And it was. They faced off for an hour. Shane got a little better, and while he couldn't match her finesse, his enthusiasm and determination made her laugh until her stomach hurt. When the twentieth song came on, he dropped to his knees and hung his head. "I bow to the queen. You win."

"Thank you, humble court jester."

He snaked an arm around her thighs and pulled her closer. She shrieked and giggled, holding onto his shoulders so she wouldn't fall over his head. Vegas was known for its tumbling acts, but her living room wasn't the best stage. He nuzzled his cheek against her stomach, and his warm breath seeped through to her skin, raising goose bumps. It might have stayed innocent, but the energy between them was too strong to ignore.

Almost of their own will, her fingers slid through his hair, and the mood changed. He turned his head and nudged the hem of her t-shirt up, placing a soft kiss just below her belly button. The tip of his tongue darted against her, and self-control was a thing of the past. She tipped her head back and gasped. Amazing how one small action could ignite her completely.

Shane trailed kisses upward, standing and taking her shirt as he went. Her bra was next. He tossed his own shirt then pulled her flush against him, and that simple but exquisite contact almost pushed her over the edge. He claimed her in a hungry kiss, his hands roaming, squeezing, caressing. He unzipped her jeans while she worked on his, and somehow they made it to the bedroom without breaking that kiss. He laid her back gently, and she pulled him with. It turned out he had more energy left after all.

Chapter Twenty-Seven

Tuesday, June 4th

Odd. Why did her bedroom smell like paper and ink? Allie cracked open an eye. Instead of her pillow, she had a close-up of her blazer sleeve and just beyond that, a fresh notepad and her pen with the cap off. Oh. She'd slept through her lunch break. She checked the wall clock. How did just ten minutes turn into an hour?

She sat up slowly with a yawn and rolled her head and shoulders. Her neck and spine creaked in a few places, and she rubbed the sore spots. It had been a *long* morning. Back-to-back appointments with the dancers after a marathon weekend of helping Miranda find a safe place when her ex got violent. The man was in jail now, but the emotional scars he'd inflicted would last the poor girl a lifetime.

Three quick knocks made her come alert just before Shane breezed in and closed the door behind him, looking grim. The fog cleared from her brain a second later, and she realized why. He opened his mouth, but she held up a hand. "Ah. If you're about to blame me for the two losses, save it. We've been through that. I can't be at every away game. I'm not necessary personnel so the team won't cover it, and I can't afford to keep flying out. And before you offer, I would feel too weird about it because turning me into a lucky charm takes away from," she gestured between them "this."

It took him a minute to process all that. She could see it in the way his expression went from determined to surprised to accepting. "A whole session in thirty seconds. That's gotta be a record. Sometimes I think we could have a complete conversation, and I wouldn't have to say a word. It's like chess to you. I can't believe you're always two steps ahead and know what I'm gonna say before *I* do."

"*I* can't believe you're not used to it yet. Now. We've established you didn't lose because of me. Why do you think you *did* lose?"

"Aww, I thought we were past this." His shoulders slumped, and he pouted. Actually pouted. Instead of sympathy, it inspired something else. She had to tear her gaze away from that full bottom lip that begged to be kissed.

"Don't think of it as doctor-patient. Think of it as a guy unloading to his ..." Really should have thought it through before starting that sentence. They hadn't put labels on anything. Though part of her wanted to, there was still that bit of resistance.

"Girl? Are you my girl?" The pleasure on his face was a real resolve killer. Hearing him say the words dimmed that resistance to a whisper. "Mine. I like that. Okay." He sat on the edge of the couch angled to face her, then blew out a sigh. "Well, Coach had a lot of ideas. Too many penalties, not enough shots on goal, weak on the power play."

"The whats and not the whys."

"Yeah. I've been thinking about that after you so gently brought it to my attention." The twinkle in his whiskey eyes canceled out any blame in that statement. "Philly got the first goal on a power play on Saturday. It was five on three, so pretty much a lock for them. I tried, but ... they were just too good at getting under our skin, making *us* go after them."

Goalies didn't usually fight, so when he said "us," it meant he saw himself and the team as one. That was good because he didn't need to take any more blame on himself. "I saw it from home. And then they got the short-handed goal."

"And it just spiraled from there. We couldn't come back. Lost our momentum. Then last night we tried to wipe the slate clean. Go in with a new mindset, but that's easier said than done. That building is overwhelming during the regular season. In the playoff finals …" He fell back against the couch and stared at the bowl of Skittles on the coffee table. "Scotty was in here. You even took out the yellow ones because he doesn't like them. Devious."

"Uh huh. Back to last night's game?"

"The energy wasn't there for us, and every time they scored, things got worse."

"That's a pretty common wall. That's why home advantage is treated like a reward. It really does have an impact. But you'll play here on Thursday to a crazy Vegas crowd, and you guys will own it."

He looked at her with suspicion. "You sound like Nealy. But nicer. Without the swearing. And threats."

"I'll take that as a compliment."

"That's your choice. But even if we win every home game, we need to win in Philly at least once to get the Cup."

"Once you prove to yourself you can beat them, it won't be so hard in Philly."

A struggling smile made its way onto his lips, tugging on her heart. "You might be right."

"I am always and undoubtedly right. You should just give in to it."

He stood, taking slow steps around her desk to stand by her chair. A wave of his cologne, and the heat of his proximity magnetically pulled her to her feet. "Will you be there Thursday night?"

She licked her lips. "Yes. But because I want to be, not because I think the team needs me."

He lifted her chin with a single finger, and his voice dropped to a low rumble. "I need you." And there went the last of her resistance, exiting in a shiver down her spine. He used the finger on her chin to pull her in for a slow, deep kiss. At first, she couldn't help but return it. The heady rush of his soft lips and gentle touch matched with the potential power and raw strength in his body was hard to resist, but finally, she came to her senses and stepped away with a gasp.

"We can't do this here."

He looked at the door. "It locks, right?"

"Shane."

"Right." He glanced back at her. "Well, I'd say tonight, but I have an early morning skate tomorrow, and then—"

"The game on Thursday. How 'bout I just see you at the game? I have an open invitation to the soccer ball warm-up, don't I?"

"Depends who you ask. Don't think Scotty liked being shown up."

"We'll just say I'm helping him conquer unsportsmanlike conduct. If he can control his temper with me, he can do it with Hartnell. Less penalty minutes for the Sinners."

"You have clearly never met Hartnell. I'll see you tomorrow." He leaned in for another lingering kiss then backed away, hands up in surrender before she could push him. "Just one to hold me over." His choirboy smile said *you can't be mad at me.*

Unfortunately, he was right.

Chapter Twenty-Eight

Sunday, June 9th

"You really won't tell me where we're going?"

"Aren't doctors supposed to have patience?"

Allie rolled her eyes in Shane's peripheral vision. "Ha. Ha. No patience on my day off."

"Well, that's unfortunate." Because they were heading to Sunrise Children's Hospital.

She squirmed around in the passenger seat to look in the back. "From the giant duffle, you're either taking me to a laundromat, or you're going to disassemble my body in the desert."

He glanced at her, arched a brow, then returned his gaze to the road. "You watch too much *CSI*."

She blew the sweep of her bangs out of her eyes and settled facing forward. "Well, you get points for not asking yet."

"Asking what?"

"Me to go to Philly for the game on Tuesday."

A reflexive denial was on his lips, but it stopped short. He *had* been thinking about it. Okay, they'd exhausted the "lucky charms had no place in relationships" discussion, but the Sinners had won over the weekend. Twice. With her there. It was hard to ignore, and it wasn't just him. The other guys seemed to take some kind of comfort in knowing the person they trusted most was cheering twenty feet away. If she wasn't a luck charm, she was at least a security blanket. Probably she wouldn't like that either, so he shut his mouth.

"Mmm hmm."

"I'm not gonna say I don't want you there. I do. The whole team does. Even Nealy noticed the difference. Don't be surprised if she asks you to be an assistant coach just so she could have you behind the bench at every game." It wasn't beyond the mighty sprite. She was goal oriented and didn't really care what it took.

Allie leaned her head back and sighed. "Once upon a time, this job was about science."

He reached over with his right hand and found hers, giving it a squeeze. "But *I* don't want to be your job. I want more than that. So I won't say a word about Philly. Though if you wanted to go, I wouldn't try to stop you."

She squeezed his hand back. That connection zinged up his arm and spread in his chest. *This is right. Undeniable.* She felt like a piece clicking in place that he didn't even know was missing.

He pulled into a space in the visitor's lot. Allie studied the building, looked at the bag in the backseat, then at him. "Are you Santa?"

"Once a month, yeah."

She smiled, then arched a brow. "Wait, why is it just you? When teams do this, they usually send three or four players. In their jerseys. With a camera crew."

The thought of that made his skin tight, and he shifted in his seat. "I don't mind the occasional meet and greet skate or charity auction, but this kinda thing … I like to go incognito. Usually on my own. Make it more about the kids than getting good press. The hospital understands and doesn't call the newspapers or anything."

Her expression softened like she was seeing him in a new light, and the look in her eyes almost made his heart stop. Maybe they weren't saying it yet, but it was there. So her next words caught him off guard totally. "Saralynn would kill you if she knew you were doing this without involving PR."

Oh damn. He hadn't even thought about that. "So we'll keep it a secret, right?"

"Secret Santas." She held up her pinky.

He hooked his finger with hers then shook on it. "Good. Now let's go. We have a lot of stops to make."

• • •

Allie followed Shane down a brightly lit hallway. The walls were covered in finger paintings and crayon drawings. The way the staff beamed at Shane from behind the nurses' desks, familiar and friendly without making a fuss, confirmed his ritual presence here, but he didn't bask in the adoration. He waved but kept focused on the children's rooms.

In the first, a little boy, maybe eight, sat in bed with a blanket pulled up to his waist and IVs sticking out of his arms. His bald head and slightly sunken eyes told her why he was there. The minute he saw Shane, he lit up with a heart-breaking grin. "Reese! I saw you win on TV!"

"That's right, Troy. I knew I couldn't let you down." Shane pulled a mini goalie stick out of his bag and a battered, plain, black puck with his signature in silver Sharpie and handed them over. "This was from the third period last night."

"Awesome!" Shock and euphoria made Troy look like any normal boy, and he pumped his fist in the air, oblivious—even for a second—of all the wiring attached to him.

Troy's father looked on gratefully from the other side of the bed. "How 'bout that, buddy? A *game* puck!"

She bit her lip hard and blinked fast. With a deep breath, her tears were under control, but no one was looking anyway. Shane knelt down and slid side to side on the tile floor, mimicking the saves he made Saturday night as Troy stared with rapt attention, and his father watched him. One save involved a dive, and as Shane rolled, his legs went up in the air, making Troy laugh and hoot, not a care in the world.

This moment was private and special, and Shane was right. Cameras didn't belong here. They talked for another five minutes about hockey before Troy waved Shane closer and whispered something in his ear. Shane wrapped an arm around the boy's scrawny shoulders and patted his arm. "You're right. I have more surprises to deliver, but I'll talk to you later, okay? You gonna watch the game on Tuesday?"

"Yeah!"

"All right, that's my guy." Shane waved, and so did Allie before following him into the hall.

She leaned close and lowered her voice. "What did he say in there?"

"Hmm? Oh. He said you were pretty. Kid's got good taste."

She took his hand on impulse. He held on tightly and kissed her temple. So natural. "You're something, you know that?"

"You save that kinda trash talk for the ice, Kally." He gave her another sweet smile before directing it to a young girl in Care Bear pajamas. "Hey, Hannah. I think I have a friend for you."

The toddler squealed and clapped as he pulled a Funshine Bear out of his bag.

Allie's heart swelled until it felt too big for her chest. *I am in so much trouble.*

Chapter Twenty-Nine

Tuesday, June 11th

Allie set the pizza on the coffee table, careful not to disturb the popcorn, pickle spears, nachos, ice cream, or chocolate covered gummy bears. "You know you have the best husband in the world."

Mac lounged back against the couch, a pickle in one hand and a nacho in the other. "Don't let him fool you. It might seem like he's covering my soccer clinics to let me have a girl's night, but in reality, you're babysitting me for free. If he had it his way, I wouldn't get out of bed for the next six months."

"It's sweet. He's taking care of his wife and baby."

"It's condescending. He thinks I don't know how to take care of myself."

Says the woman about to ingest five thousand calories in one sitting. Not that enabling accomplices had any place to judge. "He's being careful, Mac. He can't help it. But it comes from a place of love."

"You're right." Mac sighed. "Anyway, I'm yours for the next few hours. Let's see your Mr. Hot Skates give the Sinners a series lead. Think he can do it without you there?"

"He's not my—" She stopped short. It would be a flat out lie to deny he was hers.

"Ha! You can't even say it. That's progress. Speaking of which, that hospital date? You realize how big that is, right? Nobody knows he does that, not even his family. But he let you in on the secret."

True. If he'd seemed like a good guy before, that put him near sainthood. "Let's just … watch the game."

Mac snickered and reached for the pizza. She had a piece halfway to her mouth when she paused and leaned forward to squint at the screen. "Is that …?"

"Not Shane." Allie's mouth dropped open as she studied the name and number of the Sinners' goalie. Kade Simkins, the back-up, huddled in net, ready to make a save. "Nealy must have made a game-time decision. He would have told me if he weren't playing. And I'm sure I'd know if he'd been injured."

"Well yeah. You'd have been his first call. What does that mean?"

"The series is tied now. Maybe Nealy wanted to give him a break. Shake things up."

"*Now* is not the time to do that. They're two wins away from the Cup, and the Sinners dominated the last two games. Reese's play was phenomenal."

No debating that. He'd been on fire. *Not* because of her. "I don't know, Mac. Nealy works in mysterious ways. She always has a reason. It's just not usually apparent until after the fact."

"Let's hope so."

The first period was a train wreck. Simkins's stress showed in his jerky motions and delayed reactions, not to mention the horrendous rebounds. The Sinners' offense wasn't any better. They seemed spooked not being able to rely on their goaltender. The Flyers scored three times before the first horn blew. After each goal, there was a camera close-up of Shane standing by the bench in all his gear except for the mask. Even the network couldn't believe Nealy wasn't putting him in.

When the commentators came on for the period break, Mac leaned back and blinked. "Holy God."

"Yeah. That was bad." Understatement of the year. And worse? A few Sinners had looked over to the spot against the glass where she usually stood. It was stupid to feel guilty for being an M.I.A. rabbit's foot. Wasn't it? "I need ice cream." The melty tub of chocolate-peanut butter goodness helped a little.

Mac picked up a spoon and joined in. "You said she always has a reason?"

"That I've noticed. You can't argue with her results anyway."

"Oh no?"

"Okay, tonight's not the best example, but the game isn't over yet."

The junk food stash diminished rapidly during the second period. Turned out eating helped with anxiety. Her psychological training balked at that, but she kept reaching for the gummy bears. Shane was in net, thank God. He shut down the Flyers' scoring, but the Sinners couldn't buy a goal. They still looked shaky. Nealy looked angry. Some coaches hid their displeasure under a calm demeanor. Nealy was not one of those coaches. She was a wear-your-scream-on-your-sleeve kind of woman. The Sinners left the ice with heads hung at the end of the second.

"Well." Mac finished another pickle spear and licked her fingers. "I guess we know why she started Simkins. It gave Reese a kick in the ass. He hasn't played away this well all season. Too bad the rest of them can't seem to get into it."

Dave Matthews blasted and broke the silence. Allie picked up her phone, frowned at the readout, then held it to her ear. "Hello?"

"I hope you know what to do with them because I'm at my fucking wit's end. Are you watching?" The high-pitched, tiny voice was so shrill, Allie could barely hear it over the loud crowd in the background.

Mac whispered, "Who is it?"

Allie covered the receiving end and whispered, "Nealy."

Mac's jaw dropped, and she slapped a hand over her mouth.

Allie lifted her brows and shrugged. "I'm watching. The second period was a little better."

"Like hell it was. I'm putting you on speaker. Maybe they'll listen to you." The arena sounds died away, replaced with creaking benches, clunking skates, and ripping tape. "All right, ladies. I have Kally here. She has some advice for you."

I do? Her temples throbbed, and she could feel her pulse just about everywhere as adrenaline got the best of her. "Uh … hi guys."

Hesitation, then a few, *Hey Kallys*. They sounded dejected and scattered. She felt bad *for* them. One voice piped up. Sounded like Kevin Scott. "You watchin' the game?" Hope in his tone as if the idea of her watching—even from home—made him feel better.

Mac waved her arms and mouthed, *Speaker. Speaker.*

Allie gave her a look but hit the speaker button anyway. "I'm watching. First period was rough, but you held them off in the second. The third period is all about offense, okay? You can take this back. I know you can. I see their Ds are giving you some trouble and getting in the way. I can't tell you who or how I know this, but one of those guys … wears thongs. Lacy ones."

Deep laughter exploded over the phone, and she let the tension drain from her shoulders. Mac's eyes were as big as soccer balls. *Really?* Allie shook her head. Mac pulled a pillow over her face just in time to contain the cackling. Allie just hoped she wasn't going to hell for the lie.

When it seemed quiet in the locker room, she continued. "Okay? So keep that in mind and don't let them get in your heads. Win this one for me."

"For Kally!" echoed for a minute. She tried not to be happy about it. All that work detaching herself from their performance undone in two seconds. Nealy's voice came back. "All right, all right! Let's get back out there!" Excited male conversations broke out, but that only made her raise her voice. "Thanks, Kally. I'll talk to you later." The locker room noise abruptly cut off, taking her tension with it.

Mac pulled the pillow down but still hugged it to her chest. "I can't believe that just happened."

Allie set her phone by the empty nacho bowl then held her face in her hands. "Neither can I. Thousands of miles away and they're still metaphorically rubbing me for luck."

"No, I mean you *lied*. You never lie."

"I—it—I don't know. It just came out. They were intimidated. I had to say something to break the spell. It's not like I pinned it on any specific player. Just an unnamed defenseman. They needed a way to win."

"Uh huh. And any way would do? I'm not saying it's a bad thing, but I think Nealy might be rubbing off on you."

Terrifying thought.

The Sinners jumped their leash in the third period and got two goals right away. The Flyers couldn't adjust to the momentum swing and let one more goal get by before the final horn. Playoff overtime usually meant twenty-minute periods until someone scored, but unfortunately, it only took Philly three minutes and a bad bounce to take the game. Her advice *had* worked, but sometimes dumb luck trumped all. She just hoped the guys could get past it.

Chapter Thirty

"I don't know if I should do it or not. I mean, my whole life, I've wondered what my father might be like, and I wanted to meet him, but what if it goes bad? What if it does more harm than good?" Ricky sat on the office couch, twisting the end of her ponytail around her finger and studying the carpet.

It was hard to keep professional distance. Allie might have grown up with an intact nuclear family, but this kind of pain was palpable to anyone. "You said you've wondered about him your entire life. He's agreed to meet you, so chances are it'll go better than you think. And if it doesn't, you won't have that nagging curiosity anymore. It's better to know than not know. And nothing he says or does will take away from the good life you've had with your mom and stepdad. Right?"

Ricky's lower lip quivered. She sniffled and slid a hand over her nose. "You're right. Thanks, Allie." Her voice broke at the end, and a few tears slid down her cheeks.

Professional distance had a time and place, but this wasn't it. Allie sat on the couch and gave the dancer a shoulder hug. That loosed more tears, but in a few minutes, she'd cried herself out. Ricky let go to wipe her face, and Allie handed her a tissue from the desk.

Three knocks and the door opened. Jacey poked her head in. Her expression went from confused to concerned with a hint of disapproval. "Oh. Sorry. Didn't mean to interrupt." She popped back out and closed the door quietly.

Allie's skin went cold and clammy and her mouth dry. Well, the day had come. It had been a good job while she had it.

Ricky stood and finished dabbing under her eyes. "I need to get going anyway. I really appreciate you fitting me in today."

"No problem. Take care and good luck with your dad." Allie had the brief hope that Jacey had gone back to her office, but as Ricky left, the boss came in. She eased the door shut behind her and looked uncomfortable.

Jacey never had a problem with eye contact, but now she looked at the artwork, the potted plants, anywhere but at Allie. She looked like the principal embarrassed to rebuke the star student. "I'm sorry. I didn't know you were in session."

"It wasn't really an official session." It sounded lame and felt like a lie even though it was true.

"Do you counsel them often?"

"They stop in when I have extra time. The team comes first, of course."

"I feel ridiculous saying this because you're doing a good thing, but therapy isn't in the dancers' contracts. From the business side, they're part-time workers and don't have any benefits. I hate telling you not to see them, but I know how busy you've been with the team alone, and I'd rather your focus stay there. I'm sorry."

"I understand. In the beginning, Shane was my only patient, and I had a lot of down time. The dancers started coming by, and it seemed a good way to spend the day."

"Shane?" Jacey's brows went up.

Shit. No one called Reese "Shane." If anyone would be sensitive to the slip, it'd be Jacey. She'd gotten in trouble not too long ago for the same thing. "Reese. He was so happy when I helped him return to play, he said to call him Shane. Which might be the bigger miracle."

Jacey smiled, but it was tempered by the conflict in her eyes. She looked on the verge of saying something then seemed to change her mind. "Well, I stopped by to see if you were going to the game tonight. I heard you gave the guys a long-distance locker room assist on Tuesday. I think they feel better knowing you're there. Kind of like a mental health mascot. And let's be honest. Sometimes they need it. This could be an elimination game for us. I want to cover as many bases as I can."

"I'll be there. Should be a pretty amazing game. Just for the record though, you don't really—"

"Buy into the superstitious mumbo jumbo? No. I know they can win on talent alone. I also know sometimes they forget that and convince themselves it depends on something like a lucky jockstrap or the right ice entrance. Not that I'm comparing you to either of those."

"Oh, I know. I was just checking."

"Yeah. It's nice to have another sane one in the family."

Family. Allie *did* feel like she was part of the Sinners' family. But did Jacey's statement go deeper than that? Her husband was like Shane's brother, and the two men had hung out more and more since they'd cleared the air. Did Shane let something slip? While Jacey hadn't called her out on having a relationship, it seemed like she suspected it. If Allie wasn't getting the third degree, it could be because on some level, Jacey understood. If she knew officially about the relationship, she'd have to hurt people she cared about, and she clearly didn't want to do that. But Allie held no illusions. If it came down to it, Jacey would do what she must to preserve the team, and Allie couldn't blame her. Plausible deniability would work for now.

Jacey's paused with a hand on the doorknob. "You've been really good for this team. I've seen changes in all of them. They seem closer to each other. I was worried after Carter retired. Things fell apart, but you helped put them back together. We're lucky to have you."

Allie pressed her lips together and blinked back the tears that threatened. All this time after Caleb's career-ending injury, the only thing she wanted was to redeem herself—to feel like she really *was* good at this job and could make a difference. "That means a lot. Thank you. This team has been good for me, too."

"See you at the game, Allie." As soon as Jacey left, Allie hung her head and exhaled slowly. Could she sacrifice everything she'd worked for and all the good she *could* do for the possibility of love?

Chapter Thirty-One

Friday, June 14th: Game Time

Shane sat on the bench taping his pads while his teammates did the same. Not a lot of conversation, but that wasn't a surprise. Not after Tuesday night. Losing in overtime after a hard-fought third period comeback was a pretty good motivation killer, and the locker room vibe reflected it. Felt like a damn wake. Two minutes ago, Nealy and Jacey had given a *Miracle*-esque speech, and it resonated; but not enough.

The doors opened again, but now Allie came in. On a skip, as if she'd been pushed. His heart rate picked up like it did every time he saw her. She held his gaze for a second but quickly glanced around the whole room and raised a hand. "Hey guys."

A few quiet echoes of "Hey Kally" in response. Not the usual enthusiasm, because they'd let her down. No one else looked straight at her. Their loss. Her fitted black suit hugged all the right curves and made him want a few minutes alone in her office. The Lady Sinners tank top under her jacket made him grin, despite the guilt in his own gut for losing on Tuesday after they'd promised to win it for her. He focused on re-tying his skates.

"Look, I want you to know I'm proud of the way you ended the last game. You came out and dominated the third. That overtime goal was a bad bounce. No one could have predicted it. Or stopped it. But tonight you have the chance to take it back in front of *your* fans in *your* house."

The mood felt lighter as heads lifted. Scotty smirked. "You're starting to sound like Coach."

Was that a wince? "I'm hearing that a lot these days."

Shane laughed, and a couple others followed suit. Amazing how Nealy and Jacey gave a very similar speech, but coming from Allie it had a totally different effect. Not just for him. The whole team seemed to feel better; looser as they finished dressing.

"Well, I'll see you out there. Let's get this Cup!"

Barks of agreement in response, and they all high-fived her on her way out. He went last and curled his fingers around hers, holding on a few seconds longer. She took in a quick breath, and their gazes locked, so many things unspoken exchanged in that look. Very soon, they'd need to talk. Make things official. Life without her in it—*really* in it—was not an option. He let go, and she squeezed out a smile before heading for the ice. Probably she was just uncomfortable because they were in front of the team. Right?

• • •

Allie almost ran down the carpet toward the ice, needing distance from Shane and only slowing when the hulking security guard gave her a raised brow. She tried to look reassuring but didn't quite hit the mark if his wary expression was any indicator. He was the least of her problems. She released a slow breath and looked around the packed arena—a sea of black and green. Signs, painted faces, foam fingers, glow horns, Mardi Gras beads with plastic Stanley Cups for pendants. It was at once overwhelming and comforting. It felt like home.

Nowhere had felt like home since she'd left it at eighteen. She'd bounced all over the country from university to university, and those experiences had been amazing, but none of them this *right*. This team needed and loved her, and it was mutual. She couldn't lose that. But the thought of pushing Shane away, of not having him in the ways that really mattered … she couldn't do that either.

The main lights lowered and spots came on, darting around as the announcer's voice boomed. "Alllll right fans, are you ready? It's time for some Sinners hockey!" He called the starting lineup, though it was barely audible over the screaming crowd, and the guys jogged out from the locker room, bumping her shoulder with their gloves before they hopped on the ice.

The crazy pre-game energy continued into the first period. Allie pulled earplugs from her pocket. They helped dull the noise to a bearable level. It eased the throbbing in her temples but didn't do much for the knot in her stomach. The Flyers must have been able to taste victory because they didn't back down for a second. The Sinners fought just as hard, but with a tougher edge. Having your back against the wall tended to do that. When the first buzzer sounded, they were tied at one.

Without even thinking about it, she held up her fist for the guys to bump on their way to the locker room. Shane cupped the back of her head in his catching glove and messed up her hair to the laughter of the fans hanging over the railing, hoping to touch their hero. He obliged, making it hard to be mad at him. He'd just made those kids' nights.

She sighed and finger combed out the tangles, but her inner schoolgirl glowed. It was the kind of thing boys did to the girls they liked, and no one really outgrew that. Envious looks from Shane's teenage fan club confirmed that assessment. She turned toward the ice and smiled to herself.

After a hot number from the Lady Sinners and a silly, human bowling game with Sinbad, the Zambonis did their thing, and the players remerged, pumped up and smelling like a garbage strike. She held her breath while they passed, trying not to recoil when they bumped her on the shoulder.

Whatever Nealy said to them on the break must have been from *Gladiator*. They attacked, and not just with the puck. Philly's greatest strength had been to instigate fights, but the Sinners weren't even giving them the chance. They racked up penalty minutes, but unable to resist a brawl, so did the Flyers.

The tension shot higher and higher, each team getting another goal before the period ended. The guys gave her more fist bumps as they went back to the locker room, but out of ritual and not excitement. Shane didn't even look at her as he passed, but that might have been because Nealy was on his heels, her temper at a high sizzle just waiting to boil over. Allie pressed her back against the railing and closed her eyes, hoping to chameleon it and avoid the mighty sprite's wrath. She waited an extra minute to be sure before peeking. *Phew.*

A bathroom and gummy bear break later, she resumed her spot by the glass just in time. The guys shuffled by for the third period looking grim and determined as they bumped her shoulder. The Flyers came out strong and rough. As the seconds ticked by, it set in. This could be the final game. If the Sinners lost tonight, the season was over.

Nervous anxiety bubbled under her skin, and those gummy bears weren't sitting so well in her stomach. She'd started out as the team therapist, but somewhere along the line, she'd also become a fan. They were *her* team. She knew them like brothers and wanted to win as much as if she were out there herself.

Fists got in the way of scoring for most of the period. Both teams were brutal, set on winning at all costs. The announcer called one minute left in the game, and everyone in the arena jumped to their feet at full roar. Dylan Cole snagged the puck from a charging Flyer and ran with it down ice. It was so unexpected, Philly scrambled to catch him but couldn't. He faked left, shot right, and scored. The incredible cheering volume rose another two decibels, and she felt it vibrate in her chest as she screamed with them, jumping and slapping the glass.

The guys embraced on ice, touching helmets and pumping fists. They still had a chance at the Cup. The Lady Sinners and the mascot came out to dance as the team raised their sticks for the crowd. When they filed off this time, the fist bumps almost knocked her down. Shane was last, helmet in hand, and the pure joy in his face was contagious. She grinned and laughed as he picked her up and swung her around, still riding high on the moment. When he set her down, he slung an arm around her waist and bent her back for a kiss. Nothing could match the feeling. It was all passion, excitement, and euphoria, and every thought left her head.

Until the arena chorused with applause and, "Awwww."

When Shane let go, she looked around and saw them on the Jumbotron. A second later, the implication set in. It wasn't just Vegas that had seen the kiss. The whole country had.

Chapter Thirty-Two

Saturday, June 15th

"C'mon. You can't stay in there forever," Mac's muffled voice came through the comforter over Allie's head while her friend tried to jostle her out from under the covers.

"I can at least stay in here until tomorrow. And it's not like I have to go back to work." Couldn't a girl sulk in peace?

Mac yanked the comforter back and frowned. "I can't believe they suspended you."

Allie buried her face in her folded arms. "I can. I knew this would happen the minute I agreed to a date with him."

"What did they say?"

"Jacey pulled me aside right after the game. She was actually broken up about it. That's the worst part. She said she loves Shane and me, and she wants us to be happy. She thinks I'm a good psychologist and did a lot for the team. But her hands are tied. And she's right. I broke a code. There's nothing else she could have done. And she didn't say it, but the bottom line is I won't be with the Sinners for long."

Mac frowned. "Are you sure?"

She nodded.

"And Shane?"

"Hasn't stopped calling since I left the arena last night. I don't know what to say to him. I shouldn't be mad at him for kissing me. He didn't even *think* before he did it. Didn't think about the consequences."

"Kally, you know how horrible he must feel. He got carried away. Yes, it ended very, very badly, but if you kept seeing him, you two couldn't stay in the closet forever."

"I know." She sighed. "But national TV?"

Dave Matthews blasted from the nightstand, and Allie hit Ignore.

Mac pursed her lips and shoved at Allie's shoulder. "You don't think that was him trying for the thousandth time to apologize?"

"I know it was. But I'm not ready to talk yet."

"Sometimes you are too stubborn for your own good." Mac kissed her forehead then got up. "All right. We're in full wallow mode, and we'll need supplies. We finished the last of your ice cream, so that's on the list. What else?"

"Mac, I don't want—"

"Never mind, I'll improvise. I'm thinking Kahlua, celebrity mags, lots of chocolate …" She trailed off as she left the bedroom. A few minutes later, the front door banged. Blessed silence. Allie laid her head back on her arms and closed her eyes as warm tears slid down her cheeks.

• • •

Shane took a minute to steel himself before he knocked on Jacey's door. His nerves were shot, his heart hadn't slowed in two days, and anxiety felt like razor wire in his gut. He had to fix this.

"Come in."

He eased the door open and stepped inside. Jacey sat behind her desk looking like he felt. Her eyes were red and puffy with dark circles underneath. "I'm so sorry, Reese. You know I don't want to."

"Then why—"

"I can't keep her on. She couldn't treat you and see you personally. I know you've been out of session for a few weeks, but if you ever had to see her as a therapist again, it would be a huge breech of ethics. I'm not saying she came onto you, but the world sees it that way."

"She *didn't*. I went after her. I couldn't help it. I've never met anyone like Allie. She knows me better than I know myself. She challenges me and makes me own up to my own bullshit. She makes me a better man. You *know* how this feels. The thought of not being with her tears me up inside, but what's worse is knowing it's my fault she's losing the job she loved more than anything. She worked her whole life for this. Punish me, not her."

Jacey's eyes welled up. She blinked fast, pressed her lips together. "I do know how it feels. And I wish things were different. But I can't just let this slide. You're not the first here today on her behalf. The whole dance team came in this morning, telling me how much she helped them even though she wasn't supposed to. And your teammates too. They were pretty passionate about it."

"They like her better than me right now."

"That was the gist of it."

He slid a hand back through his hair. "Great."

"She may not work for the team, but you can still be with her."

"She's not answering my calls." It felt like a slap shot to the chest without pads. More than anything he just wanted to make things *right* with her, but she was shutting him out.

"I'm sorry. Normally I would say to respect her space, but I think she needs to hear what you said to me. If she really means as much as you say she does, you have to fight for her."

Oh, he'd fight for her. He just had a bad feeling she might fight back.

• • •

Distant knocking pulled Allie from sleep. As she climbed through the mental fog, everything came back and hurt all over again. She pushed the hair off her face and sat up in bed, wincing at aching joints. Who was knocking? It couldn't be Mac. She'd just come in and make herself at home.

Allie frowned and padded downstairs. She checked the peephole then set her forehead against the door. She didn't want to face him, but she couldn't put it off forever. She opened it slowly then leaned her shoulder into the frame.

"Can I come in?" He looked so somber, his usual charisma gone. The regret in his eyes sent a new aching wave through her chest.

Letting him in sounded like a bad idea, but having this conversation on her front porch wasn't an option. She stepped aside, and he angled past but stayed in the foyer. After closing the door, she leaned against it and folded her arms. "I'm sorry I didn't answer your calls. I've been … sorting things out."

"*I'm* sorry. I don't know what came over me last night. I wasn't thinking. I was so happy we got that win and you were there to see it. I forgot about everyone else. I know that sounds stupid."

It didn't sound stupid. It sounded like the most romantic thing anyone had ever said to her. And it hurt so badly because of what she had to do.

"Allie, I—"

"Shane, I can't do this. I'm so sorry." The words came out in a rush to stop him from saying what he was going to say. Even hearing the interrupted version was almost enough to steal her will. "I never should have gotten involved with a patient. I can never take it back. I gave up everything I worked for. Maybe I wasn't meant for this job. I keep making mistakes."

"That's not true. This is my fault. You were cautious but I kept pushing. You've never been anything but a good doctor." He reached for her, but she stepped back.

"I don't feel like one." She closed her eyes and gathered the courage to keep going. "I only came to Vegas for this job. If I can't find something else, I'm moving back to Pennsylvania. I care about you. You know I do. But long distance will never work."

His mouth dropped open, and the pain in his expression ripped her apart. His lips moved, but he had no response.

She pulled the door open. "I'm sorry. Please just go."

"This isn't you. You don't give up. You're too competitive. C'mon, Allie. Don't give up on us."

Her eyes watered, and her bottom lip trembled, but she caught it between her teeth. No, she didn't give up, but this wasn't a game. The consequences were already too high, and she was in too deep. The longer they tried to keep things going, the harder it would be in the end, and in her experience, long-distance relationships only ended one way.

He moved forward but paused on the front step and turned back. "Just talk to me. I would do anything to make this work."

"I wish you could." She held it together long enough to close the door and stood there for several minutes until she heard his footsteps and then his car engine before sliding to the floor and hugging her knees. The tears came, and they wouldn't stop. She cried until she couldn't breathe.

Love; this kind of love had never been on her radar. It wasn't something she'd even thought about. After her injury, the only thing that mattered was finding a way to make it right. She never could have predicted Shane. But she'd meant what she said. If she moved, they'd never see each other. Even the best intentions couldn't hold them together. As much as it hurt now, it would only be worse then.

Chapter Thirty-Three

Sunday, June 16th

Shane sat at the back of the plane with his eyes closed, a safe distance from his teammates. A few of them had a poker game going up front, while Cole and Scott played a first person shooter game on their handheld PlayStations. The rest watched DVDs on their computers. He didn't care. The only thing that mattered was they were leaving him alone. Friday night, they'd given him hell for "not learning from Phlynn." They didn't care so much about the bad press this time. They were pissed to lose their confidant and anchor. Well, so was he. Some had been sympathetic, and that was almost worse. He heard footsteps muted by carpet, and then the quiet rustle of clothes against cushion as someone sat next to him. *Go away.*

"You really gonna ignore me?" Phlynn's voice disarmed him but only a little.

"That depends. Will you go away if I do?"

"Nope."

"Didn't think so." Shane sighed and opened his eyes.

His best friend leaned back with his hands folded over his stomach. "Well, you know you won't get any shit from me."

If anyone knew how he felt, it would be Phlynn. The man had spent the better half of the previous year pretending he wasn't in love with their owner. "I appreciate that. Unfortunately, it doesn't change anything."

"Reese, I've known you for … twenty-five years?"

"Just about."

"I've never met anyone so even keeled. You were always competitive, but nothing fazed you, and no matter what happened in your personal life, you rolled with it. This year was a little different, and I understand, but then you started seeing Allie, and it was like you got yourself back. Only better. *Happier.* Without her, you're the Grinch who stole Christmas. So I'm saying this as your best friend and as a public service. Fix it."

"What am I supposed to do? If she doesn't find another job in Vegas, she's moving back to Pennsylvania. She doesn't want to do long distance."

"I could trade you to Pittsburgh."

"Not funny. Besides, they have a starting goaltender who's not going anywhere. I'm not a backup."

Phlynn raised his brows. "You actually put thought into that. You really do love her."

Yes, he did. He'd almost said it out loud, but she'd cut him off. And now he'd never get the chance to say it.

"All right, listen. You know she feels the same way about you, or she never would've risked her job in the first place. Try one more time, man. What do you have to lose?"

"Oh, I don't know. Dignity. Self-respect."

"And how much do those mean if you don't have her?"

Okay, point. Shane shrugged.

"I thought so. Get her a seat for tomorrow's game. Send the electronic ticket to her cell. Do the same with some flights. Tell her she doesn't have to come, but you want her there. If she shows, you know you have a shot. If not, you did everything you could."

"I'll give it a shot." Hope flickered, but he held it in check. Funny how losing something put into perspective just how much it meant. If this worked, he'd never take her for granted again.

• • •

Will Smith flailed around as a giant squid woman swung him back and forth. Mac laughed and pointed at the TV screen. When

Allie didn't react, Mac hit pause and angled to face her. "Okay. If a classic like *Men in Black* doesn't break through your funk, the world's slipped off its axis."

That was a pretty accurate description of how she felt. Allie hugged a pillow to her chest and set her chin on top of it. "I didn't think anything could be worse than my injury."

The joking expression slid off Mac's face, and she set a hand on Allie's shoulder. "I'm sorry, Kally. I know how much this job means to you. But you don't have to give up Shane, too. He just sent you a *Stanley Cup Final game ticket* and airfare. Do you know how many people would kill for that? He still wants to be with you."

"Yeah, now he does. While I'm here. But unless I become a showgirl or a blackjack dealer, I'll have to move back home. We'd only see each other when he played in Pittsburgh, and they're in different conferences. That's not a relationship. I don't want that for myself. And I don't want to hold him back either."

"I call bullshit. That man loves you, Allie. You know he does. And you love him too even if you won't admit it. I've never seen you like this. Even at your worst, you dealt with it by jumping wholeheartedly into another worthy cause. You know why you're not jumping this time? Because there's nothing better than what you already have. You just have to take a chance and get out of your own way."

The world went fuzzy, and sound faded away. How many times had she given that same advice, unable to believe people couldn't figure out something so simple on their own? "What if it doesn't last?"

Mac's expression turned soft, and a little sad. "Is that what you're really worried about? Or are you scared it will? Did you ever stop to think you kept dating all those Mr.-Right-For-Nows because you were afraid of the real thing?"

"That's crazy. Why would I be afraid?"

"Because you and I have the same psychological blueprint. You'd have to be vulnerable. You'd have to be on equal ground, and you've gotten used to being in the doctor's chair, safely out of reach. You'd have to give someone the power to hurt you. But the whole point is finding someone who won't, and guess what? You have."

Could the string of meaningless relationships have been on purpose? She'd been preoccupied, career-focused, busy. But busy was a symptom, not the problem. Damn. "Are you sure you weren't sitting behind me in every class at Boston?"

Mac scoffed. "My A.D.D. would never stand for that. This perspective comes from hitting the husband lottery. The proof of which is that he's picking up our Chinese take-out as we speak. I learned a lot about myself once David called me out and I stopped running. Now I get to pay it forward. Just think of me as your gentle reality slap fairy."

"You fill the role so well."

"Why thank you. Now, are you going or not?"

"It won't change anything."

Mac pointed at her. "Turn it off. The logic switch. Promise me for the next twenty-four hours you will not reason this to death. You will not analyze. And for God's sake, you will not make a list of everything that could go wrong. Sometimes you have to make room for miracles, Kally. Life can surprise you if you let it."

"You're just a walking, talking 'Hang in there' kitty poster, aren't you?"

"I'll let that slide because you're mid-wallow."

"I'm sorry. I'm lucky to have you, and I'll go. You didn't even dare me this time."

"I didn't have to. My powers are that strong."

It was crazy. It didn't make any sense. But for once in her life, maybe that's what she needed. In any case, he deserved more than what she'd given him.

Chapter Thirty-Four

Monday, June 17th

Navigating the Philadelphia airport was like playing dodge ball. Only there was no need for actual balls because the people hit just as hard in an effort to take you out if you got in their way. "So much for Band-Aids," Allie whispered under her breath. Had she lost her mind? The whole purpose of Saturday's conversation with Shane was to make a clean break. Sure, it hurt like hell at the time, but wasn't that better than watching their relationship fall apart slowly?

Past baggage claim, she stepped out of the flow of humanity and leaned against the wall by the restrooms. Even though she'd promised Mac, her logic didn't really have an off switch. But she owed Shane an apology for the way she'd dealt with things. He deserved more than that, yet the thought of drawing out the most painful thing in her life made it hard. When she brought up the Internet on her phone, her finger hovered over the touch screen keyboard, held in place by indecision. She could get a cab and go to the game, or she could just as easily book a flight home and put it all behind her.

Before she could decide one way or the other, her screen lit up with Shane's face, and Dave Matthews sang about love. The universe was not always subtle with its signs. She braced herself and hit Talk. "Hello?"

"Hey. I hear airport noises. Could that mean you're in Philly?" The hope in his voice was so clear she could almost see it.

"It could."

"Good. I'm here too."

She rolled her eyes. "Well I know *that*."

"No, I mean here, here. By the newsstand. Thought we could get something to eat before the game."

Her lips parted, and she scanned the crowd. And there he was. His back faced her, but she'd know those shoulders anywhere. She ended the call, dropped her phone in her pocket, and threaded her way through the river of people to tap his arm. He pivoted on his heel, and the relief and happiness in his face made her lightheaded. "You were so sure I'd come?"

"No. Just hoped."

Remorse and pleasure simultaneously bloomed in her chest. "I still don't—"

He slung an arm around her waist, hauled her close, and kissed her. Her carry-on dropped to the floor, and shock kept her from pushing him away. Then his free hand cradled her jaw, and the combination of tenderness, passion, and desperation left her breathless and tingling from head to toe. Heat infused the kiss slowly at first, but it quickly evolved into a blaze. His tongue dipped inside her mouth, and for a hot second, she forgot her name, let alone where they were.

Down the concourse, a baggage claim horn blared and brought reality back. Oh, yeah. Public. Airport. She took a step back and held him at arm's length. "We know *that* works between us. It won't help us figure anything out."

"You're here. That's a start," he panted with a crooked smile. It didn't quite meet his eyes. "Come on. Let's get out of here. I know a place."

• • •

That place turned out to be Lee's Hoagie House. Allie balanced a tray loaded with two giant hoagies, two baskets of fries, and two bottles of water as she made her way to Shane's table in the back. He kept his sunglasses on and head down, and so far no one had bothered him. In Philly, it was a genuine concern. They took their sports seriously, and this far into the series, they would *all* know him to see him. She set the food down then handed him the left-over change.

"Thanks for ordering. I didn't want to take any chances today. Not that I expect a physical fight, but they can be … opinionated here. And I wanted us to talk."

She slid into her seat. They did need to talk, but part of her was afraid that as soon as they did, her mental con list would exceed the positive. She picked up half of her hoagie, fingers splayed to hold it all together. She leaned in, mouth open, then leaned back and tried another angle. No point. There was no dainty way to eat the beast. She took a big bite, and tomato slime slid down her chin while lettuce rained back onto the plate.

Shane dove into his sandwich without fear of social appropriateness. It was a little like watching a hyena feed. She focused on the fries. "How'd you get away? I'm surprised Nealy doesn't have ankle monitors on you guys, making sure you don't leave the hotel before the game."

He paused, wiped his mouth with a napkin. "Phlynn covered for me. Told Coach we were going for food but he'd have me at the arena in time for warm-ups. Um … sorry about this." He gestured at the havoc on his plate. "I haven't eaten in a while."

There it was again, that pang of guilt, stronger this time because a rush of conscience accompanied it. There was no way to fix this, nothing they could do to change the circumstances. She had no right giving him hope when the end result would be the same. "I'm sorry about Saturday. I didn't handle things right. You're a really great guy, and you didn't deserve that."

"Why do I feel like there's a 'but' coming?"

"I meant what I said about long distance. I love Vegas, but I can't stay without a job."

He opened his mouth, but she cut him off.

"And before you offer to be my sugar daddy, you know I could never do that. I've always paid my own way. If I'm not going to be a sports psychologist, I have some thinking to do about my identity, but I know that it has to be *mine*. My main title can't be 'Shane's girlfriend.'" She kept her voice soft to take the sting out of the words, but he didn't seem offended.

"Give me some credit. I wasn't gonna say that. Okay, I *thought* it, but I know better than to say it. And you're not fired yet. I went in Saturday morning to tell Jacey it was my fault. She said the rest of the guys and even the dance team went in to speak for you. The whole organization loves you." The look in his eyes said he did too.

"I can't believe you all did that for me." The dancers didn't surprise her, but the guys? They weren't the most emotive group. To think they cared enough to stand up for her hit a place deep inside. They relied on her. Not just rink-side but in general. To keep their secrets. Talk through their anxieties. To understand. They depended on her, and she'd put that in jeopardy.

"It just shows what kind of person you are. Not many inspire that kind of loyalty. You can't give up on this career. It's what you're meant to do."

"I might not have a choice. It's not your fault. I made my own decisions, and the bottom line for the Sinners and any other organization is that I had a personal relationship with a patient."

"Had." A statement and question at the same time.

She sat back, any trace of hunger gone. Sitting with Mac, this wasn't how she'd imagined things would go. "I hope you know how I feel about you. I've never had this before, and I'm not saying this lightly. I regret my choices and their consequences, but I don't regret *you*. I don't regret us or our time together. I wish how I felt is all that mattered, but it's just not that simple."

"Why can't it be?" He reached across the table and held her hand. "Don't answer right now. Come to the game, and cheer us on. We can talk after."

Reason said it would be easier to end things now. Talking hadn't helped, and deep down, she'd been afraid it wouldn't. But if he went into tonight's game distracted, the whole team would lose what they'd worked all season for. Against her better judgment and all her instincts, she nodded.

Chapter Thirty-Five

Game Time

Normally, the locker room would be alive with conversation, ribbing, and laughter. There was some of that, but none around him. Whether his teammates were still pissed or just picked up on his mood, they gave him lots of space. That was fine. Shane went through the dressing motions on autopilot.

He'd gotten her to agree to talk later, but the look on her face said it all. He hadn't had much experience at being dumped. If this is what it felt like, maybe joining a monastery after hockey might be a good game plan. He couldn't relax. His stomach felt unreliable at best. He didn't take performance-enhancing drugs, so the tightness in his chest had to be heartache related, too. They'd barely had time to date. Why did he feel like he was losing someone he'd known his whole life?

Usually Jacey's good luck wish gave him confidence and made him feel good about his game, but he barely heard a word. All sound in the locker room faded to a generic buzz as he tied his skates.

"Reese. Reese?"

He blinked and looked from a jersey up to a face. Dylan Cole. The last thing Shane wanted was advice from hockey's next savior; the wonder kid.

"Ah ..." Cole looked around the room to make sure no one was paying them any special attention, then angled to sit on the bench next to him and kept his voice low. "I just wanted to say I'm sorry about what's happening with Kally. I mean, she's a great part of the team, but none of us are feeling it like you are. It really sucks, especially after what happened last year with Cap."

Funny the kid still thought of Phlynn as the team captain. It was kind of like a military or political title. You didn't lose it just because you retired. Even so, it seemed Cole still didn't feel like he deserved the position. Shane really didn't want a heart-to-heart, especially not here or now, but the effort meant something. "Thanks."

There was a little relief in Cole's face as he smiled and nodded. Did he think Shane would bite his head off? Grizzly bear temper. Another check on the break-up symptom list. The rookie stood.

"Hey, Cole. You're the cap now. How 'bout you get these guys going for the last game of the season?"

The kid grinned. "All right!" He stepped back and spoke to the whole room. "This is it, guys. The Stanley Cup is here, and it's ours. Let's go bring it home!"

Loud, guttural agreement bounced off the walls before they lined up. As usual, Shane was the last out, but Nealy grabbed his arm. His temples throbbed, and his skin went cold as he prepared to have his ass chewed out.

"Listen. You know I sympathized with Phlynn up until it started affecting his game, and then it became my problem."

She wouldn't give him shit unless he started missing saves. Message received. He nodded.

"You're one of the best goalies in the league, Reese. Keep your head in the game tonight and check your troubles at the locker room door. You owe it to your team to be present because this means everything to them even if it doesn't to you."

He looked at her sideways—a direct stare was a challenge he didn't want to make—and raised his brows. He wanted to argue. The Cup had always come first, had always been more important than anything. But she was right. He'd had a singular focus because hockey had been the only important thing in his life. Not any more. "It still matters to me."

"But she matters more. Don't bother denying it. I'm not as blind as you girls like to think I am. I hope you get what you want. But for the next three hours, I need hockey to be the only thing in your head."

He knew better than to say *I'll try*. "Try" was not in Nealy's vocabulary. There was only one acceptable answer even if he had doubts. "Yes, Coach."

"All right. Now get your ass out there. Let's win another ring."

• • •

The first period was instant mayhem. As soon as the puck dropped, so did the gloves, and both teams spent equal time in the penalty box as they did on the ice. The air vibrated with tension and promise. The weight of responsibility was so heavy, it was hard for Shane to focus on anything but the game, but that didn't stop him from trying to find Allie in the stands every time the whistle blew. She'd known better than to wear a Sinners jersey in Philly. Especially tonight. Unfortunately, her dark BU hoodie was great camouflage in a sea of orange and black. The game was scoreless when they headed for the locker room.

The guys sat, rehydrated, and toweled off. Nealy stormed in like a tiny tornado. "What the fuck was that? I love a good fight as much as the next girl, but if you're swinging fists, you're not scoring goals. Don't sink to their level unless you're damn sure you can get a power play instead of a penalty. They're playing their game and getting under your skin. You want to retaliate? Really fucking piss them off? Stop reacting. They're a rash you don't scratch. Am I clear?"

Lots of grunts, nodding, and "Yes, Coach."

They re-taped pads and sticks and got ready for the second. Again, Nealy pulled him aside. "I see you crowd-searching between plays. When I said I needed your head in the game, I didn't just mean while the clock was ticking. You were lucky in the first. There wasn't much action by your crease because your teammates were busy auditioning for WWE. You want me to put Simkins in? It would be a dream come true for him."

"No." The image of Simkins out there lifting the Cup before him tore at his pride and left a bad taste in his mouth.

"Go prove it." She slapped his back and pushed him forward down tunnel to the ice.

The second period was just as intense, but the battle for the puck replaced the physical battles. Once his teammates started ignoring the taunts, Philly got serious, and so did the traffic in front of his net. One intercepted shot led to a chance for Cole, and the Sinners lit up the scoreboard first to near deafening boos from the Philadelphia crowd. The buzzer sounded before the Flyers had a chance to strike back.

• • •

Allie flattened against her seat, trying to be invisible as the Philly fans stood booing, screamed obscenities, and waved their arms. It'd taken everything she possessed not to jump to her feet and cheer when the Sinners got that goal. If she had, she'd probably be nursing a black eye at the moment. Thank God she'd decided against wearing her Vegas jersey.

The excitement of the game swept her up, but a spike jammed in her chest when Shane looked for her between plays. At least he'd only done it in the first period. What could Nealy have said during the break? Chances were the language would make even Flyers fans blush. All of the Sinners were a lot more focused in the second, but a one-goal lead was nowhere near a guarantee.

Win or lose, she couldn't talk to Shane after the game. If he won, she didn't want to be responsible for taking away one of the best moments of his life. If they lost, she wasn't about to compound the disappointment and regret with more. They could talk back in Vegas after things had settled down. Resignation and heartache was a good recipe for acid reflux. She flagged down a bottle of water from a vendor.

The Flyers' "ice girls" were practically nuns compared to the Lady Sinners. The Vegas costumes had less fabric, more sparkle, and feathers. And they lit up. Then again, it wasn't fair to hold anything to Vegas standards. The ice girls did a cute routine and passed out t-shirts and free pizza to lucky winners in the crowd. By the time they finished, the Zambonis had laid a fresh sheet of ice, and the players returned. Shane glided to his net and slid side-to-side, etching traction in the crease. He squirted some water through his mask then looked up at her section.

Her heart broke all over again. Before she realized it, her arm was in the air, apparently of its own volition. In a crowd this big, he probably wouldn't even see her though she was only a few rows from the ice, right? Wrong. He had a laser focus in his stare, and he nodded. She pulled her arm down and glanced around, but no one had noticed the moment. Shane faced center ice, and the line of his shoulders dropped a little. Relaxed. Relieved?

The puck dropped, and madness ensued. More fights broke out, but the Flyers took most of the penalties as they grew more desperate. A sudden rush for the Sinners zone had her standing with everyone else, and when the goal horn sounded, her heart dropped. The arena roared, first in cheering then booing as officials waved off the goal. The announcer boomed it was under review, and they'd get an answer from Toronto. The whole time, she stared at Shane. His head bowed, and he rocked from skate to skate. If they lost tonight, he'd blame himself. She knew how that felt.

On ice, the ref took the mic. "After review, there was a distinct kicking motion. The call on ice stands. No goal."

The crowd outrage was so loud she clamped her hands over her ears. Her legs were ready to give out. She fell into her seat, heart hammering. Thank God. Play resumed, and the Flyers were more vicious than ever and clearly determined to take back that goal, but the Sinners held their ground. Time ticked away with a lot of close calls. The announcer thundered, "One minute left in the game!" With play in the Sinners' zone, the Flyers pulled their goalie to add an extra forward. The added rush afforded them a good shot, but Shane rebounded it. That could have been deadly, but Dylan Cole picked it up and ran for center ice. He drew back and fired an empty net goal as the last buzzer sounded.

The arena reverberated with boos. Allie clapped a hand over her mouth and screamed into her palm, wiggling in her seat. No one even looked at her. Not in the crowd anyway. Just before Shane was tackled by his teammates, he stared right at her, a giant grin on his face. She couldn't help but return it. She wanted to jump and dance, but that would get her beat up in the current climate. And in the back of her mind, she knew the euphoria wouldn't last long.

"Dr. Kallen! Dr. Kallen?" Over the quieting fan rants, a male voice reached her. The man couldn't be more than mid-twenties. Blazer over a t-shirt and dark jeans. Strawberry blond spiky hair and familiar blue eyes. Where had she seen him before? "I'm Madden Vaughn. Will you come with me?"

Madden Vaughn. That's right. His picture was on a plaque in the Las Vegas lobby. He was the Sinners' assistant GM, and now the resemblance made sense. He was also Jacey's brother. God, they weren't going to fire her right now, were they? How did they even know she was there?

She excused herself past the people in her row and followed Madden up the steps to the main concourse. Philly fans were leaving, and she had to jog to keep him in sight in the mass exodus. They came to an elevator with security guards. Madden flashed an official pass, gestured that she was with him, and the guards nodded.

The sound disappeared as the doors closed, and in the sudden quiet felt as oppressive as the large crowd. Madden extended a hand. "I'm sorry, we haven't been introduced, but I've heard about you. The team loves you, and that's an accomplishment."

She shook his hand, and his grip was firm and warm. "Thank you." She fought the urge to look away. The other half of that sentence couldn't be far behind. *The team loves you, but you loved the goalie back, so we have to let you go.* What kind of special torture was this? "How did you know I was here?"

"Ah, grapevine. Reese is best friends with my brother-in-law. It was actually Phlynn's idea to invite you. I don't know how familiar you are with what happened last year, but my sister was in a spot a lot like yours, and it was horrible."

She knew. Most of the world knew after the tabloid fiasco. "But she's still the owner of the team, and she has to do what's best for it."

He nodded.

She thought fast. What would let her be with Shane and keep her job? One answer came to mind, but it would take guts to ask for. If they were about to fire her anyway, what did she have to lose?

They reached the basement, and the doors slid open to reveal a hallway a lot like the one in Vegas. Allie followed Madden numbly.

He stopped just outside the locker room. "Wait here, okay? The guys have been through the handshakes, a couple are giving interviews, and they're lifting the Cup. I need to make an appearance too. Jacey shouldn't be much longer."

She nodded. When he left, it was a relief to be completely alone for the first time in over twenty-four hours. She released a deep breath and leaned against a cement wall. Shane had awakened something in her, touched a dormant part, and brought it to life. For the first time, it *mattered* that things might not work out. And it hurt.

The locker room door opened, and Madden ushered her inside. The quiet was broken by loud music, hooting, and yelling. She glanced around a room very similar to the one in Vegas, and "Kally!" echoed off the walls. Before she could react, they covered her in sweaty hugs and champagne.

She shrieked and laughed and tried to wiggle away, but they weren't having it. By the time she escaped, her sweatshirt was soaked, and her hair pasted to her face, sticky and sweet. Shane caught her eye. Celebration continued around them, but a bubble of stillness set them apart from it.

The next thing she knew, Jacey was at her elbow, guiding her into an attached room where players soaked injuries in ice tubs or had sore muscles rubbed back into playing shape. The party muted as she closed the door behind them. "I want to do this before things get too crazy. Allie, this whole thing broke my heart. I was always on your side, but—"

"Wait." Dizziness made her vision hazy around the edges, and she couldn't seem to swallow. "I have a proposal. I know it's a long shot, and it's asking too much, but I thought of a way to stay on with the team and still be with Shane."

The pity in Jacey's eyes was almost crushing, but she folded her arms. "I'm listening."

Not a flat out rejection. The room spun, and Allie leaned her hip into a massage table. "Thank you. The Sinners just made a deep playoff run for the second year in a row, and the team will get an influx of revenue from that. Plus, you just won your second Cup. It's enough to keep you in the black and have room to hire a second psychologist to split the load. If Shane ever needed counseling again, he wouldn't have to come to me. I've been slammed lately now that the rest of the guys have warmed up, and the dancers, they need me, too. I know it's not conventional, but … that's not really your style, is it?"

Jacey's expression remained blank, and she didn't say anything for an agonizingly long minute. Then the corners of her mouth twitched. "You sure you didn't also get a law degree?"

"No, but if that would make me a better asset to the team, I'm not above it."

"No need. You make a strong case. And you're right—I haven't done one conventional thing since I took ownership of this team. Why start now? I'll hire a second psychologist."

Allie's legs gave out, and she sat on the massage table.

Jacey winked. "I'll be right back." She disappeared back into the locker room only to return thirty seconds later with a confused Shane. Jacey nudged him with her elbow. "She's staying with us. And she's staying with you."

Shane frowned and looked between them. "I don't understand."

"Allie convinced me to keep her on and hire a second therapist."

Hope transformed his face, erased all the lines. "Are you saying …?"

"You can be together. Openly. I've never seen you so happy as when you've been with her. I'd never forgive myself if I took that away."

A roller coaster free fall rushed through Allie, but logic wasn't far behind. "Wait. There will still be backlash from the press. Not just on us but on you for keeping me."

Jacey shook her head with a smile. "When the guys came to me to plead your case, they offered to give interviews and promise on television that you were professional. They want to defend you. They garner enough respect—especially now—that it would hold weight. And as much as the world loves a scandal, they love happily-ever-afters even more."

Shane picked Jacey up, and she laughed as he swung her around. She patted his shoulders. "Why don't you save that? You know I love you, but you smell like a sewer right now."

He set her down and grinned at Allie.

Jacey wiggled her eyebrows and slid back into the locker room ruckus.

Shane rocked forward but hesitated. "So now that you can stay and we won't be burned at the stake ... do you have any other reservations?"

The cautious hope in his eyes combined with his restraint sealed the deal. He put himself out there, no safety net or walls. For her. She took two steps, curled a hand around his neck and kissed him. He returned it for all he was worth, backed her against the door, and smoothed the hair away from her face. Pure happiness and peace flooded through her and a delicious, slow burning heat. No regrets. No reservations. And no doubt that she'd finally found what she was looking for.

Chapter Thirty-Six

Saturday, September 28th

"You're up to something." Allie glanced at Shane from the corner of her eye as he drove them to the arena.

"You're paranoid." But he didn't look at her. In fact, he could barely look at her the last few days. And now he wanted her to tag along while he picked up his championship ring.

Not that it wasn't a big deal or that she had anything else to do, but something didn't jive. "You're a terrible liar. You realize I know all your tells."

He smirked and shook his head. "Just go along for the ride, Kally. Anyone ever tell you that you overanalyze?"

"I analyze just enough, thanks. It's in my job requirement." A job that had been going better than ever. The Sinners had the summer off, but training camp had started, and the influx of patients resumed with everything from pre-season jitters to girlfriend issues. She mostly dealt with the dancers, but some guys were still more comfortable spilling their secrets to her instead of the new psychologist, a nice man but a little green.

"Whatever you say." He pulled into the arena lot, parked in the underground garage and led them to the elevator. Instead of going to the business level, he hit the button for the main concourse.

She frowned. "I thought the rings were in Jacey's office."

"Little side trip."

"That's not evasive at all."

He kissed the side of her head. When the doors opened, he took her hand and tugged her toward the first section they passed, heading down to the rink. She halted in her tracks on the first landing, and her mouth dropped open. On the ice, spelled in pucks, were the words *Will you marry me?* She turned to find him on one knee and holding a little blue box.

"I told you we were coming here for a ring. I didn't just mean mine."

Vertigo swayed through her, but she managed to stay standing. Speech, however, was a little beyond her. "I … you … how …" She licked her lips. "Shane. Are you sure this is what you want?" Not that he'd given her any reason to doubt him over the last few months. If anything, they'd gotten closer and had fallen into a natural rhythm. Though, clearly he could still surprise her.

"Alexandra Kallen, I have never been more sure of something in my life. I love you. People talk about finding their other half, but it's like I found another me. With female parts. And I can't imagine spending my life with anyone else. I don't know if that's romantic or narcissistic." His brow furrowed.

She laughed and wiped a few tears from her cheeks. "Let's call it a draw." He was right though. From the day they met it had been like looking in a mirror. Maybe a circus mirror on some days, but that was normal.

"Are you saying yes?" He opened the box, revealing a gorgeous diamond on a simple band.

"Oh. Yes!"

He took her left hand and slid the ring home before surging to his feet and picking her up for a kiss. She could feel him smiling the whole time. Music filled the arena, and she leaned back. The Jumbotron read: YES!!! Applause sounded over the music, and the whole team stepped out from alcoves, clapping. The dancers too, and Saralynn (since she'd been hired full time). Even Jacey, Carter, and Nealy. And Mac. Cabbage-patching around her soccer ball sized belly.

That did it. The slow stream of tears turned into a river. Shane scooped her up again and held her tightly. For the first time since her injury, the future looked better than the past. Maybe Mac was right. Sometimes you had to make room for miracles.

More from This Author
(From *On the Fly* by Katie Kenyhercz)

Thursday, August 25th

Jacey Vaughn clutched a pile of flattened boxes and glanced around the mirrored interior of the elevator. She looked nervous, even to herself, and she swallowed, trying to wipe her slick palms on the cardboard. It felt like waiting to see the dentist. It was late August, which in Las Vegas meant temperatures in the low 90s. Even though the air conditioning hit her full blast, a bead of sweat slid down the back of her neck. When the doors opened, she took a deep breath and stepped off. Twenty pairs of eyes peered at her around cubicles, and she pasted on a weak smile. The glances followed her as she walked down the corridor to her father's office.

A petite, pixie-like woman in her late thirties darted around a desk with a ring of keys. What her light brown hair lacked in length, it made up for in wavy volume. She wore a conservative, gray skirt suit and no makeup but big jewelry. The woman smiled and looked her up and down. "You must be Jacey. I'm Nealy Windham, your father's assistant. Let me get that for you." She jiggled a key in the lock until the door swung open then motioned to the papers strewn across the desk and offered a half smile. "You can't tell now, but it cleans up pretty well. My extension is two-forty if you need anything."

Jacey braced herself, stepped inside, and Nealy saw herself out.

"Change is a good thing," Jacey whispered as she stared at the Stanley Cup Championship plaques lining the wall. They were from the eighties and the Cleveland Rockers incarnation of the current team but still reflected hockey success. The room smelled like the cedar and musk of her father's cologne with a faint undertone of cigar smoke, and she closed her eyes. She could almost feel his presence.

"Hello?"

Jacey gasped, dropped the boxes, and spun around. A man stood in the doorway, solidly built and towered quite a bit over her five feet eight inches, even though she wore heels. He wore a black Las Vegas Sinners T-shirt, cargo shorts to his knees, and leather flip-flops. His gelled blond spikes were styled to look un-styled, and almond-shaped, hazel eyes took her in with no attempt at subtlety. A small, slashing scar at the outside corner of his left eye as well as some purple-yellow bruising under his right told her who he was. Or at least *what* he was. Hockey player.

"Easy there, didn't mean to scare you. I'm looking for Mr. Vaughn."

Her heart contracted at the statement, and she took a slow breath through her nose. When she spoke, there was ice in her voice. "He passed away a week ago." Didn't they know? It was their *owner* who'd died.

The man narrowed his eyes and crossed his arms. "I know. I meant his son, J.C. Vaughn. The new owner of the team."

She bit back a smile, and her cheeks warmed. "I'm Jacquelyn Vaughn. My father ... called me Jacey."

He looked her over, but his face gave away nothing. "How much do you know about hockey?"

Jacey straightened. "I know enough. And I have an MBA from Yale, so while I probably couldn't ref a game, I can run the team. You know, I've introduced myself, but you have yet to return the courtesy."

His eyes tightened and an amused smile curled his full lips. "Carter Phlynn, captain of the Sinners."

Her face went slack then she pinched the bridge of her nose. "I'm sorry, I ... things happened pretty quickly." When she looked back to him, his sharp features softened, and his arms eased to his sides.

"I understand. I'm sorry about your father."

Jacey pressed her lips together and nodded. Carter turned to go. "Wait. You were looking for me. What did you want?"

He turned back slowly and looked at her for a long moment then shook his head. "Nothing. It can wait."

"No. Please. I could use something to take my mind off of ... "

Carter glanced to a spot on the faded burgundy carpet and furrowed his brows. "My agent was in the middle of renegotiating my contract. Your father was also the acting GM after he fired Leyman. I kind of need to know where things stand. I got an offer from the Chicago Blackhawks. My agent should be here any minute."

Jacey's lips parted as that sank in, and it took a minute to find her voice. "You want to leave the Sinners?"

He glanced at her then away again and slid a hand over the back of his neck. "I don't *want* to leave the Sinners. I've played here for the three seasons they've been a team. It's just ... Chicago is offering a better deal."

• • •

Why the hell did he feel guilty? Carter fully intended to play hard-ball and get the salary he deserved from the Sinners or walk. He'd expected to get in Vaughn Junior's face and come out with no regrets either way. The problem was that Vaughn Junior happened to have big, vulnerable, blue eyes, pouty lips, and legs for days in a skirt that showed them off. And despite the fact she probably couldn't tell a puck from a stick, there was something appealing about her.

She cleared her throat. "If you'll have a seat, I'll look through the paperwork while we wait for your agent."

Carter hesitated, but she moved around the polished oak desk, dropped into a high-backed leather chair — she looked so small — and shuffled through the piles of paper that hadn't been touched. Carefully side-stepping the boxes she'd dropped upon his arrival, he sat in a chair opposite her and leaned back, folding his hands over his stomach.

Carter took in the way her loosely curled, long, strawberry blonde hair was pulled back on top and bet she'd look hot if she let it down. Then he looked away. Hell of a thought when she was grieving for her father. He focused instead on the walls of the office, first noticing a plaque with a team gathered around the Stanley Cup. The Cleveland Rockers had been successful in the eighties but had faded in the following decades.

Next to the plaque, he spotted an old, family 8x10. Everyone in Rockers jerseys. Vaughn Senior in the middle with Jacey under one arm and a young guy under the other. Had to be her brother because they shared the same blue eyes and light hair. Jacey was smiling and happy, but her brother looked sullen, trying to be tough. Carter's eyebrows rose, but he shrugged it off and looked over the cluttered desk, noticing a gold puck with the engraving *Strive for your goals*. Vaughn Senior had certainly believed that.

"I see you've scored the most goals in the past three seasons. More than that, you've had the most assists." Her light blue eyes flashed at him, serious and ensnaring. "You're a team player; I can see why you're captain."

That sounded familiar. When it had been her old man throwing out the compliments, he brushed it off. But coming from Jacey, it sounded sincere. She ducked her head again and flipped through some more papers. If he had to guess, he'd say they were printouts of the team budget. She was actually going to be fair about this. She pulled her lower lip between her teeth and tapped a short, manicured nail against the numbers. Carter caught himself staring and wiped the smile from his face before she could see.

A knock on the open office door jerked him out the trance, and he refrained from telling his agent to leave. It would be counterproductive. Even if he did want a few more minutes alone with Jacey.

"Sorry I'm late. Previous appointment. Brad Curtis. Nice to meet you, Ms. Vaughn. I'm sorry for your loss." Brad extended his hand across Jacey's desk, and they shook.

"Thank you. I was just looking over my father's printouts and notes. From what I can tell, I'm afraid his offer has to stand. I can afford to give Carter another one point five million a year, no more."

"If you'd like to take some time — say, a week — and think things over, talk to your advisors, you can get back to me directly. Mr. Phlynn is in demand, and it would take some incentive to stay with a team that hasn't made the playoffs in its three-year existence." Brad sat in the chair next to Carter's and straightened his suit jacket.

Carter wanted to wince but kept a blank face. His agent hadn't lied about the facts, but it seemed almost cruel to lay it out for her like that.

Jacey nodded once, all business. "I understand, but I know my father. He'd have done anything to make his team the best it could be, and I'm sure that included keeping Carter." Her gaze darted to him and that damn vulnerability shone in her eyes. "If he said one point five million was the best he could do, he meant it. I know you're important to this team, and I'd hate to lose you. Will you stay?"

That question had never gotten an emotional response from him before. Not while picking his clothes up off a date's bedroom floor. Not even when his mother gave him the *my baby* face every time he visited. But damn if he didn't feel bad now. The Blackhawks' offer flashed through his mind. It wasn't so much the money. The Hawks offered him a better chance at the Cup if the past three seasons were any indicator. He glanced up to be once again pinned by that poignant stare. And before he knew what he was doing, he said, "Yeah. Yeah, we have a deal," and stood, extending his hand across the desk. Her small, soft hand felt fragile folded inside his big, callused one, and he smiled. So did she.

"You won't regret this."

His heart clenched.

"Uh, I think we should take a moment and consider — "

"Brad, I appreciate your help, but I'm staying in Vegas for at least one more season." Carter faced his agent and braced for the storm, but Brad contained it. Barely, judging from his clenched jaw and tense posture. Well, he could just deal with it.

• • •

By 6:05, Jacey had organized all of the documents into color-coded folders. Jack Vaughn's brilliance had not extended to his organizational skills. She ran a hand along the smooth, black leather of the chair and sighed. Having put her things away, she locked her new office door behind her.

Nealy stood and arched her little brows. "Can I help?"

Jacey smiled and shook her head. "Everything's finally in its place. My dad didn't decorate much, so there was room for my things."

Her assistant nodded and skirted her desk to walk beside Jacey toward the elevator.

"It took me three hours just to dig through all the papers and put them in some kind of order. If the figures I found are correct, our budget is very tight. My coach is nowhere to be found, my team captain almost quit, and in raising his salary, I've squeezed the cap even tighter. And this is only the first day."

Nealy followed, huffing a little as she kept up. "What do you mean, 'quit?'"

"He got an offer from the Chicago Blackhawks. After looking at his stats I knew we couldn't lose him, but I couldn't offer any more than my father did. If my research is right, almost *any* other team could afford to give him more, but he decided to stay with us." They stepped into the elevator and stood side-by-side as the doors slid closed.

Nealy frowned, but then a grin slowly spread, and from the corner of her eye, Jacey could almost see the light bulb go on. "What?"

Her assistant hesitated with a smug smile. "Just think about it a minute." Jacey's confusion must have roused pity because Nealy laughed. "Your father gives him the offer. He turns it down. You give him the same offer, and he takes it."

"He seemed like he really just wanted to stay in Vegas … "

"I'm sure he does. Now."

Jacey blew a loose curl away from her forehead. "That's a logical fallacy. Just because B happens after A doesn't mean A caused B."

Nealy held up her hands in surrender, but that smile was still there. "Whatever you say, hon."

The elevator doors opened to the parking garage, and Jacey paused beside her silver Eclipse. The underground air was cooler but not by much. "I can't believe he's really gone."

"Jack Vaughn was a good man and a good boss. He loved hockey, and he loved this team. But more than anything, he loved you and your brother. He talked about you every day."

Jacey felt her heart in her throat, and when she opened her mouth, nothing came out on the first attempt. The second try was a little more successful. "That's … thank you. That's nice to know."

"I know he wasn't an overly affectionate man, but he wasn't shy about his pride for you."

Jacey smiled and wiped at the corner of her eye. "Thank you. I don't know what I'd do without your help."

"S'what I'm here for. Anything you need, let me know."

"Thanks. I'll see you tomorrow, Nealy."

• • •

Jacey let herself into the hotel room she'd called home for the last week and secured the chain lock behind her. She felt along the wall for the light switch and turned it on. Her suitcases sat along the wall, neatly arranged but taking up a lot of space. Hopefully, that wouldn't be a problem much longer. Turning right to wander into the kitchenette, she opened her fridge to find the carton of skim milk and half of a wrapped, ham and Swiss sandwich. "At least there's not too much to throw away," she mumbled as she drank straight from the carton.

A little red light blinked on the phone by her bed, and she frowned. Considering her day so far, it couldn't be good. Her finger hovered over the button before she gathered the courage to push it.

"Jace, it's me. Look, I'm sorry about what I said in the lawyer's office. I just … Come on. We both thought Dad was leaving me the team. I quit my job."

Jacey rubbed her forehead and closed her eyes. "Madden … "

"The truth is, I know you can handle the team as a business. But let me help. Please. I know I've messed up in the past but … I want us to be close. You're all I have left, Jace." Her brother's voice broke on the machine, and he cleared his throat. "Call me."

BEEP.

She wandered back to the kitchenette with designs on that half-sandwich.

"Ms. Vaughn, this is Coach Tim Finley. I'm sorry to do this, but I can no longer work for the Sinners."

The milk carton fell from her hand and landed with a splat on the linoleum. She stared open-mouthed at the phone.

"Your father and I discussed my salary concerns, but we couldn't come to an agreement. I decided today to accept an offer from a different team. Like I said, I'm sorry. Best of luck with the Sinners."

BEEP.

Frantic, Jacey dug in her purse and found her cell. She searched until she found Finley's number and held it to her ear, barely hearing the ringing over the slamming of her heart. Thank God she'd thought to plug her father's contact list into her phone. As an afterthought, she grabbed a handful of take-out napkins from the counter and bent to sop up the mess.

"Hello?"

"Tim? It's Jacquelyn Vaughn."

"Ah, Ms. Vaughn. Did you get my message?"

Jacey took a silent breath and paused in her cleaning. "Yes, that's why I'm calling. Listen, if you could just coach through the next season, it would be an enormous help — "

"I'm afraid I can't do that; you'll have to find someone else."

Desperation rolled in a wave from head to toe, her chest tightened, and the wet napkins fell from her grip. "But there's no way that I'll find another coach at this short notice."

"I'm sorry, Ms. Vaughn, but I'm set on the matter."

"I understand, but — "

"I'm sorry."

Dial tone.

Jacey leaned back against the cupboards and slumped to the floor. She looked at her phone without seeing it and pushed the *off* button. After a few minutes of inaction, she set it on the counter then returned to the mess on the floor, cleaning on autopilot. An unexpected tear slid down her cheek followed by another and another. She sniffled then laughed. "I'm crying over spilled milk."

The laughter mingled with soft sobs and hiccups as she finished the job and wiped her face with the back of her hand.

She stood, kicked off her heels, and belly flopped onto the king-size bed. Face planted in the comforter, arms at her sides, and stocking feet dangling over the edge, she fell fast asleep.

• • •

Carter slid into McMullan's a little before eight. The bar was already busy with tourists and several regulars. A few heads turned, and he waved and smiled as he weaved his way to a booth in the back, where he found his best friend and goalie, Shane Reese.

Reese's baby face had followed him from pre-teen to post adolescence and guaranteed that he'd get carded well into his thirties. It also gave the goalie a female following that could rival Carter's own. Reese eyed him over a tall mug of beer as Carter slid in the opposite side. "So … ?"

Carter slouched back and took a pull from the bottle that had been waiting for him. "I'm staying."

A half smile curled Reese's mouth before he took a drink. He was one of the few men on the team with all his original teeth. A luxury of being a netminder. "Vaughn Junior bend over and beg?"

"I wish."

Reese arched his brows, and Carter smiled devilishly like a kid with a good secret. He leaned his forearms on the table and savored it for a beat. "'Vaughn Junior' wears Chanel Number Five and comes up to my chin in four-inch heels."

Reese feigned a wince. "I hope to God you're talking about a woman."

Carter laughed, nodded, and took another drink.

"And she's hot?"

A reflexive smile escaped before Carter could stop it, and Reese whistled low. An image flashed of Jacey sitting behind the desk doing mental math, and he straightened, clearing his throat. "I mean she's smart, too. Business smart, anyway. Has an MBA from Yale. She doesn't seem to know a lot about hockey, though."

"So how much more are you getting?"

Carter hesitated, shrugged and took a drink. "One point five."

"But ... " After a few seconds, the light went on in Reese's eyes. "Damn. Curtis must have shit bricks. You might need to find a new agent."

That could be true. Brad hadn't said a word to him when they left Jacey's office. "Whatever."

Reese didn't seem ready to let it go, but he did and grunted into his mug. Their plate of chili cheese fries arrived. "Peabo really cracked the whip at practice today, man. Worse than Finley. You think Coach'll show up tomorrow?"

The assistant coach, Mike Peabody, definitely had seemed pleased to take over practice. His particular style had been something like military boot camp meets Medieval torture. "I don't know. Rumor is he quit."

"You imagine that? Right before we get a new owner."

Carter only nodded.

"You gotta feel bad for Vaughn Junior too. First day on the job, her coach quits and the team captain threatens to walk."

"I didn't *threaten*. And I didn't walk. In fact, I'm taking a pay cut to stay."

Reese's smug expression said he knew why, and Carter ignored it, grabbing a few more chili fries.

"You *like* her." An accusation.

"You weren't there, okay? She had this face and these big, sad eyes, and ... "

The goalie smiled.

Carter narrowed his eyes and shook his head. "Shut up, man."

Reese laughed and finished off the fries. "Whatever. We may have been playing together since our Mites days, but you can't tell me you turned down an extra three mil just to see *my* pretty face every day."

"I'm staying. Get over it. We have bigger problems. If Finley did quit, dealing with a new coach is gonna suck."

"I hear ya, brother, but all we can do it hope for the best."

In the mood for more Crimson Romance?
Check out *Threads of Desire* by K.M. Jackson at
CrimsonRomance.com.

19385834R00128

Made in the USA
San Bernardino, CA
23 February 2015